Karin Baine lives in Northern Ireland with her husband, two sons, and her out-of-control notebook collection. Her mother and her grandmother's vast collection of books inspired her love of reading and her dream of becoming a Mills & Boon author. Now she can tell people she has a *proper* job! You can follow Karin on Twitter, @karinbaine1, or visit her website for the latest news—karinbaine.com.

Books by Karin Baine

Mills & Boon Medical Romance

French Fling to Forever
A Kiss to Change Her Life

Visit the Author Profile page
at millsandboon.co.uk for more titles.

For Tammy. From one special snowflake to another.
Our field trip was epic! xx

Special thanks to my IT guru, Cherie,
who dragged this technophobe kicking and screaming
into the twenty-first century and
managed not to throat-punch me in the process!

As always, I couldn't have told this story without help.
A big hug to my editor, Laura, to Chellie, Susan
and Alison, and an extra squishy one for Amalie
for her author guidance too. xx

Praise for
Karin Baine

CHAPTER ONE

IN VIOLET DEMPSEY'S experience the family room in a hospital department was where good news and hope came to die. It was in one of these seemingly innocuous side rooms she'd learned of her mother's fate and now she was waiting to hear of her father's too. He was fighting for his life in the cardiac care unit down the corridor while she was staring at the wall waiting for that ominous knock at the door.

She knew how crucial the first few hours after a heart attack were and she'd spent them trying to organise a flight back to Northern Ireland from London. Even that relatively short drive from Belfast to the Silent Valley Hospital in County Down had seemed like an eternity when her father was so close to death.

Their relationship was strained to say the least, since she refused to conform to her role as the daughter of an earl, but that didn't mean she didn't care. After watching her mother's struggle to fit into society life, Violet had simply decided to take her own path rather than the one her father had paved for her. They'd barely spoken since.

The tap on the door still made her jump even though she'd been expecting it. This was the reckoning. Life or death. Her stomach clenched as the door opened and the harbinger of impending doom swooped in. Except this was no po-faced stranger invading the already claustrophobic space.

'Nate?'

He was taller, broader and better groomed than she remembered but she'd recognise that dimpled smile anywhere. The hardest thing she'd ever had to do was walk away from that handsome face twelve years ago. She had no clue what he was doing here but he'd always had that knack of knowing exactly when she'd needed him.

'Hello, Violet. Or should I say *Lady* Violet? It's been a while.' He closed the door behind him and took the seat opposite her. It was so like Nate to plonk himself in the middle of her problems without a formal invitation.

'It has, but as I recall you were never one to stand on ceremony. Violet is just fine.' She hoped he was teasing her rather than trying to rile her when he understood better than anyone how much she hated her title.

They hadn't parted on the best of terms, on any terms really since she'd left without a word of explanation. Although he would have just cause to turn his back on her after what had happened, or even want a showdown to confront her about her behaviour, she was counting on him cutting her some slack in the circumstances. The old Nate would always have put her needs first and it was odd enough trying to come to terms with the fully formed man version of her childhood companion without finding out he might've completely changed character since their last meet too. Especially as she was just as attracted to Nate the adult.

The dark blond floppy hair had been tamed into a dapper short back and sides, the boyish face now defined with a sleek jawline and dusted with enough stubble to be fashionable and sexy. The son of Strachmore Castle's domestic staff had apparently swapped his hard-wearing flannel shirts for more tailored, expensive attire. He could easily have moved in her family's circle of friends now. If either of them had ever wanted that. One impulsive teenage kiss had effectively ended their friendship and sent Violet scurrying off to London before she committed to something that could never have worked.

Nate cleared his throat and she realised she'd been staring longer than an old friend ought to. The heat started to build in her cheeks as she recalled their last meet when they had ventured into new realms of their relationship.

'So… I assume you're here at your father's behest? He told me he was the one who phoned for the ambulance.' She steered the conversation, and her mind, away from dangerous territory. There was nothing like the thought of disapproving parents to pour cold water on certain heated moments that should be left in the past.

Nate leaned forward in the chair, forcing Violet to meet those hazel eyes she'd forgotten were so easy to get lost in. 'It was Dad who found him, but that's not why I'm here. This chat is of a more…professional nature. I'm a doctor here. Your father's cardiologist, in fact.'

She opened her mouth to tell him to stop messing about, then closed it again when she saw how serious he was. There was a ghost of a memory of the sister in charge mentioning a Dr Taylor but she'd never imagined this scenario in her wildest dreams.

'I didn't even know you'd gone to medical school,' she blurted out before she realised how bad that sounded. Cold. As though the spoilt brat with the privileged upbringing had swanned off and never looked back. That their time together had meant nothing to her.

It wasn't that she hadn't cared, or thought about him, over the years. Quite the opposite. She'd been afraid she'd become *too* interested in the life and times of Nate Taylor. For the sake of her new independent life away from her family's estate, she'd deemed it necessary to sever all ties with the one person who could've convinced her to stay.

'I mean, I keep contact with home to a bare minimum.' She wanted to justify her ignorance of his success in her absence. Of course she wasn't vain enough to imagine he'd spent all this time tending the grounds with his father, waiting for her return. She simply hadn't thought of him as being so…ambitious.

'I decided medicine would be a better paid, more respected profession compared to following family tradition into service.' There was that same old chip on the shoulder that had dominated conversation between them for hours in the old boathouse. Obviously their determination to branch away from the routes their parents had chosen for them had shaped both of their lives. For the better.

'You've certainly done well for yourself.' Not that it made a difference to her. Nate was a good person at heart, no matter what salary he brought home. The very reason she'd needed to create some distance between them. He'd deserved better than getting mixed up in the hell that was society life when her main goal had been to escape it.

'I'm sure I've surprised a few people round here by working my way out of a minimum-wage lifestyle. Now, I hear you've gone into nursing yourself so I'm sure you'll understand the seriousness of your father's condition.' He was definitely pricklier than she remembered and not above shaming her by displaying greater knowledge of her achievements than she had of his.

Violet's inner teenager with the schoolgirl crush couldn't help but wonder if he'd specifically sought out that information about her, or if his mother had simply been bending his ear. As the housekeeper at Strachmore, Mrs Taylor liked to keep her finger on the pulse, and that extended even as far as London. Every now and then Violet fielded prying phone calls from her father's well-meaning employee and, although she tried to keep details of her new life to a minimum, snippets of her successes and failures tended to slip through. The failures mostly related to relationships when the purpose of these communications was primarily to see if Violet had found herself a husband yet. Not in this lifetime. To her, marriage meant giving up everything you were to make another person happy and she'd seen first-hand the damage that could do. The fact she was here without her mother was proof enough it didn't work.

'Mental health is more my area of expertise.' Violet had felt so powerless after her mother had taken her own life she'd wanted to train in an area where she could make a real difference. It could be a challenging role at times but one that brought its own rewards.

She was doing her best to emotionally save lives, if not physically like Nate.

That little nugget apparently was news to him, as his raised eyebrows finally gave an indication he felt something more than indifference to her.

'I guess that's…understandable and admirable.'

The compliment was hard won. Not that Violet had chosen her profession to gain brownie points from anyone, but Nate seemed reluctant to give her credit for getting off her backside to work instead of languishing in that house. It was another reminder they'd left those summer afternoons planning their escape far behind.

'Us kids done good.' For old times' sake she decided to praise them both for doing exactly what they'd said they would and breaking free from their parents' hold.

Although, her father would've been appalled by her murder of the English language after paying for her elocution lessons. That was exactly why she'd relished doing it so frequently during her adolescence. Credit where it was due though, those hours spent improving her pronunciation had probably made her transition to London easier than sounding like a Northern Irish Eliza Doolittle. Perhaps she owed the old man some credit even if it had felt as if he was trying to force her to be someone she wasn't at the time.

'And yet here we are…'

She knew he was trying to get her to focus back on what was happening here and now but the words held a different meaning for her. No matter how hard she tried, she would never be able to completely separate her world from her father's.

'Okay, give it to me straight. Is he going to make it?' At some point she was going to have to apologise for running out on him but that would mean having to explain why she'd done it. It wasn't the time or place for that intense personal conversation, given the reason they were both here.

The scowl marring Nate's brow was further indication that her father was as bad as she'd feared. 'As you know, your father has suffered a myocardial infarction—a heart attack. He was unresponsive when the paramedics arrived and they had to resuscitate him on scene.'

It was no wonder Mr Taylor's message had been so fragmented and frantic. Technically, her father had died. She really didn't know how to feel about that. Since her mother had passed away Violet had resented him—for the way he'd treated her and for not being the one to have gone in her place. Now she was faced with the possibility of losing him too, things didn't seem so clear-cut. When you stripped away the bad memories and anger, he was still her father. She was starting to understand why her mother hadn't been able to simply walk away when the going got too rough. Sometimes having a conscience could be a terrible thing.

'A heart attack,' she repeated. Even though she'd heard it from others, coming from Nate somehow made it more real.

He nodded. 'It's been confirmed by blood tests. The increased levels of cardiac enzymes have indicated the presence of damage to the heart muscle. We'll continue taking bloods every six to eight hours as well as running electrocardiograms, ECGs, to monitor his heart's electrical activity and make sure there are no further complications. The next twenty-four to forty-eight hours will be crucial. Our first line of treatment would usually be emergency angioplasty to widen the arteries and allow easier blood flow to the heart. Unfortunately your father has proved…opposed to that idea.'

Nate didn't sugar-coat it. He didn't need to. They both knew she preferred straight talking to well-meaning platitudes. That way she wouldn't get hurt by hidden truths further down the line. Such as finding out her mother's overdose hadn't been as accidental as she'd first been led to believe.

It was a typical response from her father to ignore advice and insist he knew better than everyone. This time it could cause his own death instead of someone else's.

She closed her eyes and took a deep breath, batting away those old feelings flooding back and that helplessness at not being able to shake her father into facing facts. It hadn't worked for her mother so her chances after all this time were slim.

'Do we know what caused it?' She knew nothing of his lifestyle these days but she doubted his love of whiskey and cigars had diminished since she'd last seen him. He was a man who did as he pleased and sod the consequences.

'There's no family history of heart disease that we know of and no current health problems, I understand. We'll know more after we run a few tests. For now, our priority is limiting the damage to the heart.'

'I'm sorry I couldn't give the nurses any more information.' She grimaced, imagining the low opinion the staff were already forming of the absent daughter who couldn't give them any insight into her own father.

'It's all right. I understand things have been…tricky

between you both. We've pieced together what we could in the meantime.'

No doubt the Taylors' close relationship with her father had played a part in gathering that information. Violet didn't begrudge the bond the families had, but it sometimes made her feel inadequate, superfluous to requirements. Indeed, no one had ever needed her until now. Even now she wasn't sure how her presence would be received by either side of the class divide.

'Can I see him?' No matter how fractured their relationship had been since her mother's death, or how frustrating he was, he was the only family she had left. Just because she wasn't the daughter he wanted didn't mean she'd stopped caring about him. It simply made it more difficult.

Nate bounced back up onto his feet. 'I might be able to pull a few strings and get you a couple of minutes with him.'

The way he'd been reacting to her she was surprised he was willing to do anything other than list the facts of her father's condition. She figured this one must be for old times' sake—the days before things had got complicated and she'd made him despise her.

Determined to make the most of this breakthrough, she followed him into CCU, bobbing up and down like a meerkat keeping watch for predators as she tried to locate the patient. Nate strode through the ward with an air of confidence and authority she'd never seen in him before. It suited him. She had a sense of pride in him as patients and staff alike sat up straighter as he walked by. Finally people other than her had realised his worth in this world.

She zoned out the blue flashes of nurses zipping by

and the hospital beds occupied by ill strangers to hone in on her father. He was in the top left-hand corner of the room, by the window. At least he'd only have one immediate neighbour to complain about when he was back to his grouchy self. The Earl Dempsey would not be happy to find himself on an NHS ward surrounded by the great unwashed when he woke instead of some private hospital he'd happily pay through the nose for. Tough. When all was said and done, Nate and his colleagues were all that was keeping him alive.

'He's a little out of it at the moment due to the morphine we've given him to reduce the pain.' Nate led her to the bedside and for the first time in her life Violet felt sorry for her father. The man who'd virtually driven her mother to death in the pursuit of gaining a higher status in society now looked like any other old man lying there in his hospital gown, his white hair matted to his head and tubes and wires covering every inch of him.

She couldn't miss the monitors charting his vital signs, the IVs pumping life-saving drugs into his system, or the oxygen mask keeping him breathing, but she didn't cry. Nate's shoulder was safe from her tears these days. That display of emotion was reserved for the privacy of her own home where no one could witness her weakness. There was no way she was going to end up like her vulnerable mother, letting others take advantage of her. She was stronger than that. She'd had to be.

'What are his chances?' Violet was so matter-of-fact, so devoid of emotion, Nate was concerned she might be in shock and he'd have to treat her too. Then this night really would be complete.

Until now, he'd only seen her act this coldly once before. He knew she hadn't visited home since leaving for university but this was still her father lying here on the brink of death. The girl he'd grown up with had years of fear and hurt built up inside her because of this man, whether she loved him or not. There ought to be some sort of reaction to finding he could die without ever resolving the past.

He'd held back from saying those things that had sprung to mind the minute he'd known she was in the building, all of them prefaced with 'why?'. He'd had no choice but to pick himself back up and get on with life after her disappearing act but that didn't mean he'd stopped asking himself what he'd done to drive her away.

Seeing her again brought conflicting emotions to the fore. That broken-hearted teenager who still haunted his relationships would probably always hold a candle for her but with that came the hurt of her abandonment and that dismissal of his feelings for her.

Instead of acknowledging his declaration of love for her, or reciprocating, she'd walked away and refused to see him again before she'd left for London. It had been the only time she hadn't turned to him for advice, or confided her plans. The only time she'd turned her back on him instead of leaning on him for support. Although her rejection had cut him deeply, he'd tried to turn it into a positive. If he'd carried on in that vein, as an emotional crutch for her, he would've remained stagnant at Strachmore in his parents' footsteps. They'd given the best years of their lives to the running of the castle, sacrificing everything else in their loyalty to the Dempseys.

Despite his father's view that they owed the family some sort of non-existent debt that included tying the next generation of Taylors to the Earl's needs, Nate had sworn not to get drawn into that trap. His parents might have conceded some of their freedom to maintain their positions but he was pretty sure sacrificing their firstborn hadn't been included in the terms and conditions of their contracts. This was his life, and he'd had ambitions beyond the Strachmore estate.

Violet had been the one flaw in that plan. He'd probably have given up all of his hopes and dreams to be with her. It still hadn't been enough. *He* hadn't been enough. Her actions had been confirmation he needed to do something with his life beyond the estate and he owed her for giving him that final push. That was partly why he'd insisted on speaking to her himself tonight.

He'd often imagined the moment their paths would cross again. Every medical exam he'd taken and passed with flying colours had been his way of getting his own back, proof he had been worthy of her after all. He mightn't have been born into money but with hard work he'd earned it, along with a good reputation. She would've seen that for herself if she'd shown any faith in him and stuck around.

There were many points in his career where he'd been spurred on with the thought of being able to flaunt his success some day. As if she were a loser in a game show and he were showing her what she could have won. If money and status had been all that mattered to her when he'd only had love to give, he knew she'd be kicking herself to find out he had it all now.

He'd be lying if he said he wasn't curious as to how the years had treated her too. If her mother's death had changed her emotionally, life in London had certainly transformed her physically. Although she'd hate it, her noble heritage shone through in every step she took. The once waist-length raven hair was now styled in a sleek bob, and her skinny frame, although still slender, definitely had curves in all the right places. She was every inch the sophisticated woman about town even in her casual butt-hugging jeans and silky polka-dot blouse. However, her new look and altered attitude couldn't hide the real Violet from him. Those blue eyes, the colour of a stormy winter's night, were as troubled as ever and he couldn't bring himself to confront her about the past when she was already in such turmoil.

It could wait until they were both ready to talk and stop pretending seeing each other wasn't a big deal. She might've moved on, consigned everything they'd had together to the past, but he still needed an explanation as to why she'd turned her back on him so he could close that chapter. Violet's rejection had marked the one failure in his life and that wasn't something he found easy to live with.

Although he wanted answers, for now he'd have to put his personal feelings aside and treat her as he would any family member of a critical patient. In the old days he wouldn't have thought twice about throwing his arms around her and giving her a much-needed hug, but they weren't here together through choice. Neither were they angsty teenagers united in rebellion against their parents. They were adults, virtual strangers who knew nothing of each other's lives. He chose a clinical approach to appease this edgier version of the girl he once knew and try to maintain some sort of professional distance from the case.

After dealing with the Earl, he had a renewed appreciation for what Violet and her mother had contended with. The frustration at not being able to do his job and perform the angioplasty because of his patient's non-compliance had made him want to scream. In some ways he understood Violet's decision to leave him to his own devices; it was easier than standing by and watching him self-destruct. Even in the jaws of death he thought he thought he knew better than those around him. As if he imagined continued denial would somehow defy fate.

'He's not out of danger yet but he is in the best place. We've administered clot-busting drugs quite early so it should restore the blood flow and reduce the damage. In my experience, the earlier we treat the patient after a heart attack, the better chance of survival they have.' Although he performed this procedure day after day, it was never routine. Every patient was individual, reacted differently to medication, suffered varying degrees of muscle damage and experienced all sorts of complications on the road to recovery. All he could do was fight with all the drugs and technology he had available to him and the rest was up to fate, or the stubbornness of the patient.

'I don't wish him any harm, you know. Despite everything. I'm not heartless.' Violet leaned across the bed and for a split second Nate thought she was going to reach out to her father. At the last second she withdrew again.

'I know. I'm sure he knows it too.' He might have had his doubts about that when she'd abandoned her life here with him in it, but she'd proved that rumour wrong by simply being here. Clearly she still cared for her father, and Nate had no doubt somewhere deep down the feeling was mutual. The trouble was they were both too stubborn to make the first move on building that bridge. He'd seen how the loss of her mother had affected Violet and he dearly hoped there was still time for her to connect with her father, to get closure if nothing else.

Nate had had his own parental issues but he still checked in with them on a regular basis. He just made sure he kept enough distance to ensure they didn't interfere in his life and he didn't get roped into drama at Strachmore. Until now.

The steady blip of the monitors suddenly flatlined as the Earl's heart rate dropped. Nate swung into action as the alarm rang out to summon the crash team. A second arrest was always a possibility when patients were at their most vulnerable after the first. Especially when they'd refused life-saving treatment. In Nate's head he'd thought bringing Violet in could somehow prevent the worst from happening. Instead, she was here to witness it for herself.

'Violet, I'm going to have to ask you to leave.' He motioned for help to get her out of here. Saving a man's life wasn't as pretty as they made out in the movies and he certainly didn't want family members in the audience for the performance.

'Nate?' She didn't have to say anything else. The

trembling bottom lip caught between her teeth and wide eyes expressed her plea eloquently enough.

'I'll do everything I can. I promise.' He was forced to block out that haunting image of her silently begging him to save her father so he could focus on the job at hand. He didn't want to be the one to have to deliver that earth-shattering news to her for a second time.

Sweat beaded on his forehead as he charged the defibrillator that had been wheeled to the bedside.

'Stand clear.'

The first shock Nate administered to try and kick-start the heart again was for the Earl, and Violet, and a second chance for their father-daughter relationship. He started CPR, thinking of his own parents and their ties to this man with every chest compression.

So much for not wanting anyone relying on him. Now both of their families were depending on him to save the day. And a life.

CHAPTER TWO

NATE LEANING OVER the bed, pumping her father's chest, was the last thing Violet saw before the ward doors swung shut, closing her out of her father's struggle for life. A nurse steered her back towards the cell she'd vacated only minutes earlier for another interminable wait. With her pulse racing, her insides knotted, she didn't have it in her to resist a second incarceration.

There was nothing she could do but take a seat in her still-warm chair. Everything was in Nate's hands now. Literally. She trusted his word to do his utmost to save his patient; he'd never let her down before. It had been the other way around. When he'd kissed her, told her he loved her, she'd run away rather than confess she felt the same. It was the one thing she couldn't give him, dared not give him, when she'd watched love destroy her mother.

She admired Nate's professionalism after the way she'd left things with him. There was an aloofness about him she wasn't used to, but she guessed she'd been the one who'd created that by going to London without telling him why. Perhaps it was water under the bridge for him and not something he was keen to be reminded of. In fairness, she probably deserved a lot worse than the cold shoulder and she didn't think she'd be quite so civilised if the situation had been reversed. Whatever his thoughts on seeing her, she was grateful to him for not calling her out on what had happened. She didn't want to deal with any more emotional fallout today. For someone who did her best to keep her feelings on lockdown, this had been a doozy of a day already and she couldn't face any more demons from her past.

Yet, here she was relying on him the same way she had every time her parents had fought, feeling sorry for herself and wondering what the future held. This time her thoughts were consumed with becoming an orphan at the age of thirty instead of being married off to another family who valued reputation above all else.

There was a tentative knock on the door and the same nurse appeared with a tea tray. 'I thought you could do with a cuppa.'

'Thanks.' Violet accepted the offering with a forced smile. Despite the fact she hadn't eaten anything since receiving that fateful telephone call, her stomach was in too much turmoil for her to even face the plain biscuits presented to her with the tea.

'You need something to keep your strength up. You'll be no use to your father if you faint from hunger.'

Violet honestly didn't know what use she'd be to her father whether she was conscious or not, but her new shadow stood waiting and watching until she took a nibble at a biscuit and a sip of tea. Only then, her care of duty fulfilled, did the nurse leave her alone again.

The next time the door opened some time later, it was Nate who entered. She told herself the little flip her heart did was in anticipation of finding out her father's fate. It had absolutely nothing to do with the sight of Dr Taylor with his shirt sleeves rolled up and his perfectly groomed hair now ruffled and unkempt as if he'd just got out of bed. It was clear neither he nor her father had had an easy time of it.

'We got him back.' Nate immediately ended her suspense and she let go of the breath she'd been holding since he walked in.

'Thank you.' Her voice was nothing more than a whisper, her throat burning from the tears she couldn't shed. Until today she hadn't realised how much it meant to her to know she wasn't alone in the world.

'We'll keep him under close observation. A second arrest was always a possibility after the stress his heart has been under today but he's stable now.'

Nate's dedication was a blessing. Especially when her father had treated him with nothing but disdain when they were growing up. He thought associating with those below one's station was degrading and it had been to blame for Violet's 'rebellion'. In hindsight, she wondered if he'd seen how dangerously close they'd come to having a proper relationship and that had coloured his view of their friendship. Nate would never have lived up to her father's idea of a noble son-in-law to carry on his title. Not that he would've wanted it either. He hated Strachmore as much as she did. In the end the Earl's campaign to keep them separated had been a wasted exercise on his part. Violet had no intention of settling down with anyone, whether she loved them or not.

'Thanks for keeping me in the loop. I know you're probably needed elsewhere.' She was under no illusion that this particular cardiologist was assigned to her only. He'd undoubtedly done her a huge favour by personally informing her of her father's condition. For reasons known only to him when he'd made it clear he hadn't forgiven her for her sins.

'Do you need me to order you a taxi? Is there somewhere you need to be?' He eyed her small *I-left-in-a-hurry* luggage, probably keen to ship her out of his territory as soon as possible.

She'd barely packed enough for more than tonight, but that had been out of sheer panic rather than optimism.

'I'm fine here for the night if that's allowed? I can pull a couple of chairs together.' She hadn't thought beyond getting here before it was too late, never mind overnight accommodation. Since it was still touch and go, her personal discomfort didn't seem that important.

'You can't sleep here. I'm sure you're exhausted.'

There was a pause and a heavy sigh before he continued. 'I'll give you a lift back to Strachmore and get the keys from my mum to let you in.'

Nate sounded resigned to homing her for the night, as if she were a stray dog he'd picked up on the side of the road and was stuck with until help arrived. This was how things had always been between them—Nate finding solutions to problems of her own making. Except back then he'd always seemed to enjoy coming to her rescue.

'Honestly, I don't want to hold you back any longer. I'm sure you have other patients to see and this means I'm close if anything happens during the night.' If she was honest she wasn't sure her family home would be

any more inviting than this windowless broom cupboard.

Nate dipped his head, looking decidedly sheepish.
'My shift finished hours ago. I'm all yours.'

A shiver played across her skin, teasing every tiny
hair to attention. It was her guilt at keeping him at his
post through some misplaced sense of loyalty manifesting. Definitely not a physical reaction to him offering herself up to her.

'I can't ask you to—'

'You didn't. I'm volunteering.' He was already grab-
bing her bag and robbing her of her refusal even though
he made his offer sound as if he'd had no other choice.

He paused by the door and fixed her with those
soul-reaching eyes. 'The night staff will phone you,
and me, if there's any change. I'll get you back here in
a flash if it comes to it.'

'Only if you're sure?' She'd finally run out of excuses not to go home.

Violet waited in the car while he paid his parents a
visit. She hoped it was quick. The longer they were
travelling companions with this elephant from the past,
the more likely they were going to have to acknowledge it. She wasn't ready to face that, or the Taylors.
Not that she held any ill will against the pair—after all,
they were the ones who kept this place running—but
she was tired and definitely not in the mood for grand
reunions or lectures. Nate had left the engine running
and the heater on so he clearly didn't intend to loiter
either. He was probably every bit as eager as she was
to put today behind him.

She shifted in the leather bucket seat, which was

marginally more comfortable than the hospital waiting chairs. The mode of transport she was being chauffeured around the countryside in was still something of a shock to her system. To see the boy who'd spent his summers working umpteen jobs to save cash had splashed out on a bright red sports car was more surprising than if he'd turned up on an ancient motorbike and sidecar. It was almost as though he was sticking two fingers up at everyone who'd treated him as a second-class citizen in his youth and told him he'd never amount to anything beyond Strachmore. Ironically, the youngest member of the Dempsey family relied on public transport to get her from A to B. It was more practical for city life but it also had the added bonus of ticking off her father.

She watched Nate stride back to the car in the muted evening light. He could easily pass as the master of the big house now he'd swapped his ripped jeans for those tailored suits. Although, he would probably look good in anything. Or nothing.

Whoa!

Those teenage hormones she'd thought she'd left behind long ago had apparently resurfaced and mutated into adult ones. It had been a long, emotional day and clearly she was misinterpreting his reluctant kindness for something…sexier.

She cleared her throat as he opened the car door and climbed back into the driver's seat. If only she could clear her mind of the images she'd planted there as easily. Her wayward thoughts weren't helped by the fact his tall frame was packed so tightly into the car, his thighs were almost touching hers.

'Mum's in a tizzy about not having the place cleaned

for your arrival. I assured her I'd roll the red carpet out for you myself but we'd best get out of here before we run into a cleaning mob brandishing mops and dusters.'

Violet ignored the barb, simply grateful he'd run interference for her, when Mrs Taylor was probably bursting with questions for her. 'I'm sure the house is as spotless as ever with your mother at the helm. I only wish I could clone her and take her back to London with me.'

Unlike Strachmore Castle, her poky flat was never going to make the cover of any magazines but she worked hard to pay the rent. That meant more to her than gleaming silver and polished marble floors ever would.

Nate threw the car into reverse and rested his arm along the back of her seat as he kept watch out of the back window. The smell of soap and hard-working doctor enveloped her and for a moment she was tempted to snuggle into his solid chest. He could give her comfort and a whole lot besides. Exactly why she should stick to the idea of him as only a friend, or her father's doctor, and not someone who'd taken the lead role in her first erotic imaginings.

'Do you know how long you'll be staying? I mean, is someone holding the fort for you while you're here?' He trained his eyes back on the dark road leading from the cottage up to the main house, so Violet couldn't tell if he was fishing for personal info or making polite conversation.

'I'll stay as long as I'm needed. I have a lot of personal leave I can use.' She preferred to keep busy with work rather than take duvet days where she had nothing to do but dwell on things beyond her control. It wasn't the first time her superiors had warned her of possible burnout if she didn't take a break from her caseload so they'd be only too happy for her to take some time off.

'If you need anything my parents will be here to help.'

He was leaving himself out of the equation but it was a long time since Violet had relied on anyone having her back. For good reason. She'd needed to learn to stand on her own two feet to make herself stronger than her mother had been.

'Thank you. I know you've gone out of your way to help me and I wouldn't want to get your other half offside by holding you hostage to my problems.' Okay, she *was* fishing. He'd been her first crush, her first kiss, it was only natural that this curious cat was wrestling a green-eyed monster at the thought of him going home to another woman. One who wasn't afraid to make compromises.

'There's no danger of that. I'm a confirmed bachelor.'

Those words had the same effect as if he'd thrown a bucket of ice-cold water over her as she jumped from one conclusion to another. She'd been so caught up in her feelings for him she'd never contemplated how much his could have changed for her, or for women in general. Suddenly his new grooming regime started to take on a whole new meaning. 'You're not—'

'No, I'm not gay, Violet. I thought you of all people would realise I'm attracted to women.' He turned and, though Violet couldn't see his face clearly in the dim interior, she imagined he was looking at her lips, remembering *that* kiss too.

She'd managed to block it out for over a decade but

here, so close to him again, it was all she could think about. That first tentative exploration of each other had soon given way to a raw passion she hadn't experienced since. These days she approached any romantic entanglements with a certain degree of cynicism and caution, which meant she was always holding back. In that moment with Nate's lips on hers she'd given no thought to consequence or complications that could arise. That had come later when she'd tried to imagine a future together and failed. He didn't belong in her world and vice versa. Ironically they seemed to have traded places anyway.

As the stately home loomed into view of the car headlights, the butterflies in her stomach turned kamikaze, dive-bombing her insides until there was a chance she might hurl over the expensive leather upholstery. At least it was wipe-clean.

'Home sweet home.' Nate's attempt at humour was a welcome distraction from the memories assaulting her from the second the stone pillars of the eighteenth-century house came into view.

Her father, spit forming at the corners of his mouth when she defied him by sneaking out to a concert with Nate.

Violet hiding in the old servants' quarters when she was supposed to be dining with the Montgomery family, whose son had been deemed a suitable match for her at the age of seventeen.

The empty pill bottle by her mother's bedside.

Dark humour was definitely the cure for dark memories.

'In case you can't see it, I'm giving you the death stare.'

Nate gave a hearty chuckle, letting the serious doctor mask slip for a glimpse of her old friend. 'Nostrils flaring, mouth puckered up like you've just licked a lemon, eyes narrowed to mere slits—I can picture it now.'

Violet flattened her lips back into a thin line with a huff. She could hear the smugness in his voice that he still knew her better than anyone even after all of this time.

They pulled up into the driveway and the sound of the handbrake meant there was no more stalling.

'Thanks for everything. I can let myself in.'

'No can do. I told you I'm under instruction to escort Lady Violet inside her ancestral home. Don't forget, under different circumstances I could've ended up as your official errand boy.'

He was being facetious. Violet knew he would never have played the skivvy any more than she would've been the boss lady. Still, it conjured up more interesting images if they'd chosen different paths.

She let out a long sigh and admitted defeat. Having a surly Nate here was infinitely more bearable than having Mrs Taylor fussing around her, or setting foot back inside alone. It was one thing going home to an empty flat at night but an entirely different game coming back here where the ghosts of her past roamed the hallways.

Nate really needed to work on that keeping-at-arm's-length ethos where relationships were concerned. He'd thought he'd built up a tolerance to all things Dempsey since his teenage heartbreak. One glimpse of those big blue eyes and he was taking on the duties of the whole domestic staff who'd once resided here—the chauffeur, the butler and housekeeper all rolled into one. He told himself his promise to light a fire and see her settled in was the only way to keep his parents at bay and Violet's discomfort to a minimum. They meant well, their subservient role so deeply ingrained in them the very thought of Lady Violet returning to a cold, empty house brought them out in a cold sweat. He knew this would be difficult enough for her without an audience and he still had a duty of care via her father.

Despite their history, or possibly because of the one they'd had pre-kiss, he still felt an obligation to help her. Perhaps he wasn't as far removed from his heritage as he liked to think. He'd really been the only one Violet had had to turn to when things had got rough and it would be callous for him to abandon her now for the sake of his own pride. He simply hadn't been able to leave her for the night in that waiting room, expecting her to bed down where she stood. In a fit of madness he'd even briefly contemplated taking her back to his house rather than expect her to face this place alone.

Ultimately he'd done enough damage to his relationship boundaries already. She was only back in the country five minutes and he'd already landed himself firmly in the friend zone. Not a position he wanted to be in with any beautiful woman. Especially one he already had an emotional history with. One who'd dumped him without a second thought. Then there was the double blow to his ego with the whole gay thing. He knew one teenage fumble probably hadn't made a long-lasting impact on her but he'd assumed it had been enough to define his sexuality.

Now he'd slipped back into a supporting role there was no way he was ever going to win top billing as Violet's leading man. If he'd once imagined taking her back into his arms and replacing that inexperienced make-out session with a more confident approach to recover his male pride, he'd stuffed up the minute he'd insisted on staying to talk to her about her father. Friends or lovers—there was no in between for him when it came to the women in his life. He didn't even want to peek inside people's personal baggage, never mind help them unpack it, and yet that was exactly what he was doing now. The pressure was on him more than ever to save his patient and return everyone back to their normal status quo. As soon as he'd done the gentlemanly thing and seen her settled in, he could walk away with a clear conscience. He'd proved the better person by not exacting revenge.

'You put the kettle on and I'll get the fire started.' He opened the heavy front door with a reverence the stately home deserved even if the current owner didn't. It was a beautiful building, full of history and wonder. Unfortunately it also held negative connotations for those entering it tonight. While Violet had been the princess held captive in the tower, he'd very much been the lowly serf kept in his place by his master. He'd dealt with a lot of those issues through hard work and determination but he couldn't help feeling Violet still had to face hers. Although he still had an axe of his own to grind with her, he wasn't totally unsympathetic. It was best he try to make this as normal as possible for her. As if they were walking into any other family home and not the country pile of her ancestors. Easier said than done when there was a huge chandelier dominating the space in front of them.

'We do have modern-day conveniences like central heating.' She was still resisting his attempts to phase her into her surroundings gradually with his assistance, but he was used to dealing with difficult patients and bolshie family members.

She was more defensive than he remembered. He guessed years of independent living had toughened her up. A definite plus given his aversion to needy people outside the workplace.

'And kettles?'

It amused him to watch her flounce away the way she used to when his teasing went too far. It was further proof her fiery spirit was very much alive. She was going to need it to see her through the next days, whatever they held.

'Milk, no sugar,' he called after her as he headed for the study.

It was the closest and smallest room on the ground floor, and easier to heat. The pale blue walls and ornate white ceiling of the entrance hall were pretty and in keeping with the period pieces dotted throughout but they didn't make the cool atmosphere any more inviting. Okay, they had no practical need for a fire but there was something homely about a real fire. It was cosy and welcoming, something this house was sadly lacking.

He could sense the disapproving stares of past earls staring down at him from the walls as he trespassed into the inner sanctum. They all had the same stern features of Samuel Dempsey. Nate wondered if not smiling was another one of the house rules Violet had deigned to disobey. Ruling with an iron fist might have worked in the olden days but, as far as he'd seen, all it had succeeded in doing in recent times was shatter the family.

'Is this where they found him?'

He hadn't heard Violet enter the room as he'd knelt to set the fire in the hearth. It wasn't until he turned around again that he understood why she'd sounded so pained.

Her father's papers littered the mahogany and brass writing desk and spilled onto the floor, his chair toppled over in the corner of the room with a whiskey tumbler lying next to it—the contents of which had seeped into the antique rug long ago.

'I'm so sorry, Violet. I had no idea. We can move into the drawing room and I'll get this tidied up.' Regardless of the painful history between them, he would never have purposely exposed her to this scene. He took the rattling cups and saucers from her shaking hands before she slopped the tea on the expensive furnishings too.

'It's all right. It was just a shock.' She righted the heavy chair and Nate set down the tea things so he could help.

They both bent down to reach for the upturned glass at the same time, Violet's bracelet clinking against it in the process. He reached for her wrist, curiosity getting the better of common sense.

'Is this the one I bought you?' It was only a cheap turquoise bead bracelet with a dainty seahorse charm hanging from it. So unlike the diamonds and pearls her mother had favoured on occasion. He was surprised it had stood the test of time, even more so to find she still wore it.

A trace of a smile lifted the corners of her mouth. 'Yes. From the day at the aquarium.'

The day things had changed between them for ever.

'You were fascinated by those damn seahorses.'

She'd stood for ages watching them as if she'd found her peace there and he'd wanted her to have a souvenir of that summer afternoon together. He hadn't known it would be their last.

'They're just so…serene. I envy the simplicity of their life. And, of course, it's the male who gives birth. The female seahorse has a much freer life than most women, she transfers her eggs and goes back to her own place—the onus isn't on her to carry on the family line.' It was a tragic narrative of Violet's childhood when she'd been jealous of a fragile species trapped in a tank. At least now she was free of some of her burden even if it had cost Nate a piece of his heart in the process.

He flicked the charm up with his thumb so it rested on his nail. So small, so inexpensive, so evocative. If that day had meant nothing to her, if he'd meant nothing to her, why would she still be attached to it now? He felt her pulse quicken beneath him, met her eyes with his, and they were back in that bubble where nothing mattered except the chemistry.

He didn't know who'd leaned closer to whom but suddenly they were no more than a breath away from kissing. Violet's eyes fluttered shut, her lips were parted and waiting for him. There was nothing he wanted more in that moment than to give into temptation. Despite how much she'd hurt him in the past, he'd wanted to do this the minute he'd seen her again but this was typical Violet behaviour. She couldn't drop him and pick him up when the mood took her. Not any more. Especially when she still hadn't done him the courtesy of an apology or an explanation, never mind simply acknowledging what she'd done to him.

Unfortunately physical attraction couldn't always override common sense. A kiss was much more than that when it was with your first love, the woman who'd broken your heart without a backward glance.

He let go of her wrist and stepped away from temptation. As he began to collect his thoughts away from her lips, the Earl's collection of antique clocks chimed the late hour and sounded the death knell for this… whatever the hell it was.

When he didn't swoop in and ravage her, Violet was afraid to open her eyes and face him. She'd done it again—gone with her heart instead of her head. Thank goodness one of them had been thinking clearly this time. She shuddered at how close she'd come to making another monumental mistake when she'd yet to address the last one she'd made with Nate. Her world was complicated enough now without resurrecting old emotions like zombies wandering through her life with no real purpose except causing eternal misery for everyone in their path. She needed to remember that every time she was tempted to lose herself in his embrace, that one place she was able to forget her troubles.

In her defence she'd been under a lot of pressure today and Nate had been her one source of comfort, the only familiar thing from home that didn't make her want to run screaming. Even in his current indifferent state. She blamed her faux pas entirely on stress. Apparently making moves on hot doctors was a side effect of tangled emotions no one had warned her about. They hadn't covered that in her course. Then again,

Nate was the professional—he should've known he was in danger simply by being in the room with her.

In fact, he seemed to have found the best treatment for her particular case by continuing to pick up the debris around them and ignoring the latest addition to the elephant herd now parading around the room.

'No wonder Mum was so frantic about getting this place tidied up before you set foot inside. I guess they just locked up the house once the ambulance left.' Nate in cleaning mode was as efficient as his mother and Violet decided to follow his lead. Time and distance hadn't made this any more feasible.

They worked quietly together, sifting her father's correspondence into manageable piles. The quicker they got this sorted, the easier it would make it for Nate to leave. She knew him well enough to know he'd see this out until the end, when he'd fulfilled his obligation to her and his parents.

'Violet?' After some time he drew her attention to a stack of letters headed with bold red lettering.

'Mmm?'

'These are all bills. Most of them final demands.'

'Let me see.' She snatched a few from his grasp and confirmed it. All correspondence, most of it threatening action against him, was leading to the conclusion her father was in dire financial trouble.

She collapsed into the chair with such force she almost toppled it over again. This was too much for her to handle on top of everything else today. Somehow she was going to have to fix this. She just had no idea how.

'You had no clue this was going on?' Nate spoke softly, as if he was afraid of spooking her even more.

The façade her father had presented to the world all these years had duped many into thinking their fortune was never ending. She'd known differently.

'The place has been leaking money for years but I didn't know things were this bad.' Her father's spending and refusal to admit they were in trouble had been the source of many an argument in the house before her mother died. The worry and uncertainty about the future had certainly contributed to her mother's fragile state of mind but he hadn't taken any responsibility then and he wasn't likely to do so now.

'What? There's no magical pot of gold hidden under the floorboards?' Nate pretended to be surprised the place didn't run by reputation and superiority complexes alone.

'Unfortunately not.' She lifted the stack of bills and slammed them back down on the table. This wasn't his problem. Hell, it wasn't even hers.

Whatever happened to her father, Violet knew she was going to have to be the one to sort this out. She should have known better than to come back. It had been inevitable that she'd get sucked back into her father's delusions of grandeur and the repercussions of stark reality. Perhaps she should have done as she was told at seventeen and agreed to marry Lord Montgomery's son. At least she might've been in a position now to help financially, possibly with her mother still around too.

This new discovery threatened to undo all the progress she'd made in her new life. Nothing had changed in her absence, she'd simply avoided dealing with it. She was back to being that frightened girl, lonely and overwhelmed by the burden her father had put upon her.

She wanted to confront him, scream and cry, and walk away for ever. Now she could do none of those things. She was stuck here. Again.

'I'll worry about these tomorrow, as soon as I know he's made it through the night. Then I might go up there and kill him myself.'

Nate arched an eyebrow at her with a smirk. 'Now, I know you don't mean that. I told you, there's help available. It's a shame you Dempseys are too damn stubborn for your own good. You don't have to do this on your own.'

Deep down she knew he was talking about his parents or some other official source of financial advice but it gave her more comfort to imagine he was still in her corner. 'You're the only person who was ever there for me, you know.'

Reuniting with Nate was the only light in this darkness and she wanted to run towards the safety she knew was there. For a little while she didn't want to think about tomorrow, or the next day, or the next. He could help her forget, take her to that happy place away from all of this mess. What was one more mistake when her life was crumbling around her? All she had to do was convince him, and herself, this wasn't the big deal it had been when they were teenagers.

Suddenly she was tired of being strong, of bearing the weight of Strachmore on her shoulders alone.

'Stay with me tonight, Nate.'

Nate's body reacted to the invitation before his brain kicked in and listed all the reasons this was a bad idea. He ignored all parts of him straining to make the decision for him, knowing Violet would regret this in the morning, as he would. For altogether different reasons. This was his chance to exorcise that painful rejection for good, but he knew her well enough to understand what this was really about. Her way of dealing with difficult matters had always been to divert her attention elsewhere, put off tackling the hard stuff for as long as possible. Violet was the Queen of Procrastination and he'd always been the Fool, keeping her entertained and distracting her from the hardships within the castle walls.

Not any more. He'd made certain he was King of his own castle since those days.

'I think it would be better if I went home.'

She'd let him know he wasn't good enough for her before and he wasn't going to be the consolation prize now.

She stood up so she was close enough to invade his personal space and trailed a fingertip down the front of his shirt. 'Don't tell me you haven't thought about this, about us—'

She didn't need to say any more. He was already picturing them together in bed, giving into that chemistry he'd never been able to forget.

He took a deep breath to purify his thoughts and make sense of hers. She'd taken an emotional battering today and he'd never take advantage of her when she was so vulnerable. Lord knew he wanted her and it was an ego boost to know it was reciprocated this time but it didn't change circumstances. *Friend or lover?* He reminded himself he couldn't be both and remain sane. He'd breached the professional boundary long ago and only friendship had remained before he'd ended up in no-man's land—a minefield he had to tiptoe through, full of the sort of explosive situations he'd happily avoided since he was nineteen.

'We're both adults, single, with no illusions this would be anything more than sex. I need the distraction.' It was confirmation of exactly where he stood with her and that wasn't any place of importance. She might as well have been hiring an escort for the evening for all the emotional significance she afforded him.

Normally that kind of detachment wasn't a problem. In fact he welcomed it. It stopped things becoming too messy. However Violet wasn't a faceless one-night stand. Uncomplicated sex should never involve the woman whose rejection had made you so cynical about relationships in the first place.

'Unfortunately, sharing a bed is not the modern-day equivalent of hanging out in the boathouse pretending real life isn't happening around us.' His heavy dose of honesty transformed Violet's coquettish eye-fluttering into a wide-eyed, open-mouthed, I've-just-been-slapped-in-the-face expression.

He was pretty sure he'd worn that same look once before and he took no satisfaction in being the one to cause it this time.

'You're right. I don't know what the hell I was thinking.'

He could see the shame clouding her eyes already. That wasn't what he wanted either.

'There's nothing I'd enjoy more than taking you to bed right now, but I think it would be a mistake. For both of us. Get some sleep and I'll see you in the morning.' He knew she didn't want to be alone, but he didn't intend falling into that old pattern of being at her beck and call again. He'd invested too much in that before and paid the consequences.

'You always were the sensible one.' She gave him a wobbly smile and Nate knew he had to get out of here before the tears really did fall. When she finally did give into the real emotions she was trying to hide from, he knew he'd never be able to leave her.

'And you always were the impulsive one.' He'd lost count of the number of times he'd had to talk her out of doing something stupid—like running away or sabotaging her father's dinner parties with laxatives. It was probably the reason she hadn't confided in him about moving to London. She hadn't wanted to be talked out of it.

This proposition was most likely a cry for help rather than an unyielding need to have him in her bed, but it didn't make it any easier to resist.

'Goodnight, Violet.'

He wondered if she'd ever regretted walking away as much as he did now.

CHAPTER THREE

THE TROUBLE WITH the countryside was the quiet. There was no traffic noise to drown out Violet's thoughts and nowhere to go to escape her shame. She'd spent most of the night replaying the moment she'd made a complete fool of herself with Nate. Lord knew what he thought of her throwing herself at him like some nympho desperate for a quick lay. She shuddered, the cringe factor at an all-time high as she recalled the look of disgust on his face as he rejected her advances. All he'd done was show her some kindness, more than she deserved, and she'd implied she was only interested in his body. Nothing could be further from the truth. Well, okay, his body had been on her mind since she'd first seen him suited and booted but she'd needed him for so much more than that. She'd tried to use sex to get him to stay when she was really yearning for his company.

After one bombshell too many, her common sense had been blown to pieces. There was no other logical explanation for her behaviour last night. These past years of being so strong, so independent had skewed her idea of friendship until she'd seen it as a weakness. Until yesterday, when Nate had reminded her how good it was to have someone in your corner fighting your battles with you. In her messed-up head, sleeping with Nate had seemed like the only way to recapture that fantasy world they'd had when they were young but he'd called her on it. She had no right to expect anything from him when she'd been the one to burst that bubble in the first place. What had been the point of walking away then if she was simply going to drag him back into all Strachmore's problems now?

In the cold light of day Nate's refusal to stay had probably been the most sensible option but her ego was still a little bruised. Clearly he'd done what she'd ultimately wanted for him at the time and moved on from her. She should be happy about it. Not wondering what, apart from her badly executed proposition, had turned him off her. That one kiss had been so full of love and passion for her she hated to think she'd killed it stone dead with her actions, even though she'd acted in what she'd thought was in both of their interests.

At least *not* sleeping with Nate meant minimal embarrassment when she would inevitably run into him again. The good news this morning was that her father had made it through the night and was as well as could be expected for a man determined to be in control of his own destiny at any cost.

Now that the sun was up she was keen to get to the hospital and see him but her thoughts were as muddled as ever when it came to her father. Last night she'd been afraid for him, and herself, as far as his health and finances were concerned. Yet there was also that lingering resentment that he'd brought her back here, unintentionally or not. These rose-covered walls and four-poster bed might be the stuff of little girls' dreams but to her this had always been a prison, a place that had robbed her of her freedom. Even as an adult she was still trapped here.

She tossed off the covers and climbed out of bed, her bare feet sinking into the thick wool carpet reminding her she wasn't in Kansas any more. The wooden floors throughout her flat served a dual purpose—minimum cleaning and a stand against her old-fashioned upbringing.

She wandered down the halls trying to find the beauty in her opulent surroundings and failing. The shiny, gilded trinkets and ornate antiquities were exquisite but at what cost? She would've taken a childhood in a one-bedroom council flat if it had meant she could've had her mother back. Not so her father. Even when his wife had begged him to downsize to stem their outgoings, he'd refused to part with the family silver or make any concessions to give her peace of mind. If anything, he'd become more extravagant, throwing lavish parties to prevent the rumour mill churning with stories about the depleted family coffers. Her mother had been expected to be compliant in the façade, playing the glamorous, gracious hostess while quashing her anxiety with a cocktail of drugs.

Violet slid her hand over the smooth mahogany bannister leading down the staircase. It took her to a happier period when the house was her playground and this was her slide taking her from one floor to another. With few friends outside her preparatory school, she'd had to make her own entertainment when she'd been waiting for Nate to finish working in the grounds with his father. At least with him she'd never had to pretend to be something she wasn't. She shouldn't have tried to do that last night by making out she was some sort of good-time girl.

Perhaps he'd seen right through her façade the way he'd always been able to and realised she'd simply been acting out of fear. That thought was preferable to the one where he didn't find her attractive any more and enough to spur her on to get dressed and face the day ahead.

So many elements of what happened last night had been playing on Nate's mind. The most persistent one being Violet's indecent proposal and why he'd turned her down. He doubted she felt any more for him now than she had back then and surmised she'd been trying to use him as a sticking plaster over the wound coming back here had reopened. He knew he'd ultimately made the right decision. Going down that path again would only have led to that same dead end it had taken him years to navigate his way out of.

In hindsight her flight to London rather than take the next step with him had probably been for the best. Nothing had changed since then. Except they were no longer best friends and self-preservation was a higher priority for him now.

The discovery of the Earl's debts had added to his disturbed sleep; he was worried not only for Violet but for his family too. Regardless of his own thoughts on Strachmore, or the people who resided there, his parents were very much a part of it. Any financial problems would affect them too when it was their livelihood, and their affiliation was the only thing keeping a roof over their heads. The cottage was the only perk of the job as far as he could see and one that would certainly vanish along with the Dempseys. Strachmore's problems were also his now. He couldn't stand by and watch his parents lose their home simply because he and Violet had unresolved issues. They were all going to have to work together to find a solution. The future was going to have to be more important than the past.

He'd made Samuel Dempsey his first port of call on the ward rounds this morning to follow his progress. All had been quiet since the last dramatic intervention to restart his heart so Nate hoped this was the start of his recovery. There was no associated arrhythmia, with the heart beating too quickly, too slowly, or irregularly, which could sometimes occur after a heart attack. It would take a while to assess the full damage done to the heart and how much tissue would be able to recover but, for now, he was stable.

That was more than could be said for another one of his elderly patients, who'd suffered severe heart failure and had undergone stenting of his coronary arteries yesterday. The balloon catheter supposed to inflate/deflate timed by the patient's heartbeat and support the circulation hadn't been beneficial in this case. After examining him, Nate had had to concede that a large part of the heart muscle had died and nothing more could be done. A younger patient might have been a candidate for further surgery but it had been decided at the morning multi-disciplinary meeting not to pursue any further investigation. Already weak, the patient wouldn't have survived another round of intrusive surgery. It wasn't the outcome he wanted for any of his patients, no matter what their age or circumstance. He absorbed every loss as though it were personal, his failing. If anything happened to the Earl he'd never forgive himself for letting Violet or his parents down.

After seeing in-patients, outpatients and performing a pacemaker insertion, he'd come full circle back to CCU. Deep down he'd known Violet would be here.

'Hey, Dad.' Violet was glad to see he was a bit more with it and his pallor was a lot less grey today. She'd been sitting around for hours waiting for all the tests and scans to be completed before she got to see him. Making her own way to the hospital this morning had seemed like a better plan than car-sharing with the man who didn't want to sleep with her but it also meant no string-pulling visitor privileges.

'Violet? What are you doing here?' His eyes were flickering open and shut as though he wasn't sure whether or not to believe what he was seeing. It was no wonder when she'd spent so long out of the country, and his life.

'The doctors have told you what happened, right?' She didn't want the responsibility of breaking the news to him; he wasn't invincible. He'd probably call her a liar if she tried.

'A heart attack.' He nodded and closed his eyes again. She couldn't tell if he was tired, zoned out on drugs or annoyed she was here. Probably all three. She was the last person he'd want to see him weak and out of control.

'I wanted to make sure you were all right.' It was weird saying that when she'd barely let him enter her thoughts until recently. He'd been out of sight, out of mind, to enable her to move forward. Until one phone call had forced her to acknowledge he was still part of her life whether she liked it or not.

She stood by the bed, arms folded and doing her best to sound strong, as if admitting she'd been scared for him would somehow give him power back over her.

'I'm grand.'

And people wondered where she got her stubborn streak from. There was no point telling him how close to death he'd come. He knew. He simply wouldn't admit it to her or himself.

She waited for something more—a complaint about sharing a room with the general public, a request for water, an acknowledgement of what it meant for her to be here. Nothing. Not even an attempt to keep his eyes open.

Violet took deep breaths to try and quieten the urge to treat this as some sort of therapy session, unleashing years of unresolved issues in a verbal tirade while he was strapped down and forced to listen. He was still a sick man and she was living with enough guilt without having to shoulder the blame for his possible relapse. She'd waited this long, she could hold out a little longer to say her piece. Preferably when he and Strachmore were back on their feet and she'd bought a return ticket to London.

'And how are we doing today, Lord Dempsey? You were asleep when I came by earlier.' The sound of Nate's voice close to Violet's ear made her jump. Lost in her inner raging, she hadn't heard him approach, hadn't expected him to purposely come within five hundred yards of her after last night.

Even while she was trying to find the courage to face him her cheeks were burning. Looking him in the eye after her epic seduction fail was akin to watching your drunk antics at a wedding back on video. Except she didn't have alcohol to blame for losing control of her mind and there was definitely nobody getting married around here.

'I feel like I've been hit by a truck, Doctor.'

Violet could only shake her head in disgusted wonder as Rip Van Winkle bypassed her with the truth in favour of the medical professional. It said everything about their lack of communication and trust.

'Your body went through a lot yesterday so you are going to be quite sore for a while. We'll give you some more pain relief to make you more comfortable in the meantime. I don't have a problem with you calling me Nate if you prefer, Lord Dempsey.' He was smiling as he reached for the chart at the end of the bed with no obvious signs of long-lasting trauma after her little display last night. Things could've been awkward but he apparently wasn't going to make an issue of it. Not in public at least.

'Why would I want to do that?' Her father was making an effort to sit up now, scowling as he did so.

Violet's stomach sank with the realisation he didn't know who it was who had saved his life. Nate deserved some sort of recognition. 'You remember Nate, Dad? Bill and Margaret Taylor's son? He's a cardiologist now.'

'For now we need you to rest but as soon as you're feeling up to it we'll need to get you moving, even if it's just to sit in the chair by the bed. It's important we get the blood flowing around your body again.' Nate ignored her attempts to big him up and went about his doctory business.

Violet couldn't help the eye-rolling when she might as well be talking to the walls today for all the notice anyone was paying her. Perhaps she'd actually died of embarrassment when Nate had walked out last night and this was actually her ghost standing by the bedside whom no one could apparently see or hear.

'Nathaniel?' He was peering at Nate, his face screwed up in a sneer. Yeah, the penny had finally dropped.

Nate gave a curt nod. 'There appears to be some narrowing of your arteries, Lord Dempsey, and we will have to look into the possibility of a surgical intervention before they become blocked again.'

'You had a lucky escape this time, thanks to Nate.' She wanted to fend off the vitriol she could see was already building with his strength.

'I want to go home.' There was no thanks or recognition this man had saved his life, only demands.

Violet didn't know why that should surprise her. Owing his life to someone he'd looked down on for most of his life would mean admitting his stereotyping had been wrong. That chaos theory would rip his entire belief system apart. It was about time.

'I'm afraid you can't just yet. We need to build up your mobility gradually so you don't overdo it. Trust me, we want you recovered and out of here as soon as possible too. We need the bed.' Nate still managed to crack a joke even though it was probably killing him as much as her not to bite back.

'And when you do, you're going to have to cut back on the whiskey and cigars, Dad.' It was time he took responsibility for his own actions to save his own skin if no one else's.

'Just like your mother. Trying to tell me what to do. Who asked you to come back here anyway?' The old curmudgeon closed his eyes and lay back down. Conversation over as far as he was concerned.

Violet's blood was boiling. All anyone had tried to do was help him and all they ever got in return was verbal abuse. The olive branch she'd held out was being whacked around her head with every dismissive utterance.

'This is for your own good. If you don't want me here, if you don't want Nate involved, then start looking after yourself.' In all the years she'd spent with her own patients, she'd always been able to tread carefully and keep her temper in check in the toughest circumstances. Right now it was stretched to snapping point. There'd been a very good reason she'd left her personal baggage in a different country—it made her a different person. A weaker one.

He didn't bat an eyelid.

'This is something we can discuss once your father is up to it. Lifestyle will be something we'll cover during rehabilitation. I think we should let you rest now, Lord Dempsey.' Nate addressed her directly for the first time since he'd sneaked in and it was to undermine the stance she was trying to take here.

She swung around, hands on hips, and tried to communicate via the medium of dirty looks how ticked off she was with him. The patient gave a grunt next to them, which Violet knew amounted to another dismissal. The chance to get everything off her chest had passed and she wasn't best pleased about it.

Nate did his own spot of mime, nodding towards the door. She had no option but to follow when he turned on his heel and walked away from the volcanic eruption she was building up to. She didn't attempt to quieten the fast click of her footsteps out into the hallway after him.

'What?' She was mad at him, her father and, most of all, herself for ending up back in this situation.

He held one hand up in surrender, with the other resting on the door handle of that dreaded family room. 'Can we talk?'

'Not in there.' She was already on the edge without being forced to relive that nightmare again.

'That's right. It'll be safer for me if we go somewhere more…public.'

She heard the tease in his voice before she noticed the glint in his eye and the dimples blossoming in his cheeks. It was too hard to stay mad when he was giving her his best 'naughty puppy' look. Violet groaned in defeat. It had been too good to be true to think he would let last night's shenanigans sink without a trace.

'What can I say? I was clearly in the midst of some sort of breakdown. I promise not to try and jump your bones today. I'm sure there's some sort of medical ethics involved where you're not allowed to bring that up without my permission.' The only blessing about this continued humiliation was that, by turning it into a joke at her expense, they'd broken the ice before it had time to fully form between them.

She was loath to admit it but she needed him as a friend if nothing else. It was one thing being strong and independent when you were able to leave all of your troubles at work, quite another when they followed you home at night and invited their mates round to party. A familiar, if not overly friendly, face was the only thing stopping her from being completely overwhelmed and jumping on the first plane back.

'That really only applies if you're my patient...'

'I'm sure with the stress I'm under that's a definite possibility. So, if we can forget that ever happened... you wanted to talk?' If her father was going to continue playing dumb she was going to have to get back to Strachmore and make a start on that pretty red paper trail. She knew she wasn't going to like what she found at the end of it.

Nate gestured towards the empty plastic chairs in the corridor. It wasn't exactly the cosiest set-up for a heart-to-heart but there was every possibility she'd break her promise if they were holed up in that confined space again together. That white doctor coat suited him. It said he was in charge and that was irresistible to someone whose own confidence was floundering more with every second she spent back here.

'First off, I wasn't trying to interfere in there. I know you have a lot of things to sort out with your father but it's going to have to wait.'

She was so intent on watching his lips and imagining how differently things could've turned out last night, it took a few seconds for his words to register. 'Sorry. What?'

'We need to keep his stress levels to a minimum while he recovers. The lectures can wait until we get him through the other side of this. Trust me, we'll be giving a few of our own on his lifestyle before he leaves.' He rested his hand on top of hers, probably the way he offered his support to all family members who walked these hallways. Violet wondered if his touch had the same effect on them. The bolt of electricity shooting through her at the point of contact was powerful enough to make the heart defibrillators redundant.

She slid her hand out from his so she could think clearly. 'You're asking me to back off?'

'For now, yes.' He could just as well be talking about the inappropriate thoughts she kept having about him.

Back off. Stop picturing me wearing nothing but my stethoscope.

She reluctantly agreed. The strength of her willpower would surely be tested over the next few days. In both areas.

'Now, I don't want to tread on your toes any more than I already have but I was thinking about Strachmore.' His scowl seemed only natural. It pained Violet every time she thought of the place too.

'Did the nightmares keep you awake last night?' She thought he appeared a little more rugged this morning and had hoped that spurning her advances had kept him awake with regret.

Oh, wait. That had been her.

Nate gave her his version of the death stare. It didn't have the same menacing effect when he puckered his lips at her. She was simply tempted to help smooth them out again.

'I'm serious. I had a few ideas of what you could do to generate some income.'

'I'm listening.' So far her only plans had included selling up or torching the place for the insurance money. Both of which had her conscience screaming 'Cop out!' She'd probably find herself haunted by the ghosts of past earls for eternity if she surrendered their legacy so easily. Besides, she was none too fond of playing with matches. There was always a chance of getting burned.

'Okay, so, I was thinking more long-term financial stability. A way of making the estate self-sufficient. You have beautiful gardens, large banqueting areas and floors of empty bedrooms. It's the perfect wedding venue. Stately homes are all the rage these days and not only for receptions. You can apply for a licence to actually hold the ceremonies on site—' Nate had obviously given this a lot of thought in the space of a few hours. No doubt it was a ploy to get her out of the country quick smart before she put him in any more awkward situations.

'That sounds…complicated.' She rubbed her temples, the mere thought of tackling this bringing on another tension headache.

'Perhaps, at the beginning, but once everything is in place I'm pretty sure the bookings will come flooding in.' He made it sound so simple.

'Where do you even begin with that sort of thing?' It sounded like a lot of hard work that would keep her here far beyond a couple of weeks' paid leave. She didn't want to start something she'd be expected to see through to the end. Her idea of helping was to get the bills paid while her father was laid up, not take on a whole new set of problems on his behalf.

'You'll need public liability insurance for a start, and then the licences for alcohol, entertainment, et cetera. There'd have to be a fire-risk assessment, maybe some planning permission depending on how far you want to develop this.'

'I'm not sure I do. I'm not sticking around, remember?'

'I know. I'm just brainstorming ideas that will keep the place afloat so you don't have to come back.'

'Of course.' Violet took a direct hit in the feels. This wasn't Nate trying to ease her burden. He just didn't want her hanging around.

'You don't have to jump right in at the deep end. There's no reason why you couldn't test those waters first by opening the place up to the public. You could run tours of the house or hire out the gardens for photographic shoots. There's endless possibilities.'

And an infinite number of new headaches to deal with.

'I suppose it's worth looking into.' Especially if it meant she could absolve herself of further responsibilities or reasons to return. Coming back had only managed to upset the new life she'd created for herself and Nate had made it abundantly clear there was nothing left for her here. If only this weren't such a Herculean task to take on herself it could've proved the answer to all of their prayers.

'I've spoken to my parents and they're on board with whatever decision you make. After all, Strachmore is their home too. There's just one problem…'

'Of course there is. You're sure it's just the one?'

'Well, one particular obstacle which could shut the whole project down before it gets off the ground.' The way he was fidgeting with his tie gave away his sudden nerves, which didn't bode well for Violet. She thought he was supposed to be bringing her solutions, not more reasons to get wound up.

'Which is?' She sat on her hands so she didn't give into her instinct to stick her fingers in her ears. She had to hear this if she was to find some way out of this whole mess.

'Your father. We'll need his say-so on everything.'

Not even Nate's apologetic smile could salve that slap in the face.

The man who'd let the castle crumble around him was the only one who could save it. If he weren't so completely blinkered by his self-importance there might've been a chance that plan might've actually worked.

'That's the end of that, then.' Enough people had wasted their time and energy trying to wake him up to what was happening around him for Violet to know this was a lost cause.

'I get this isn't going to be easy but it'll be worth it in the end. You'll finally be able to leave Strachmore behind.'

She couldn't fault his logic. It was the lack of emotion she was having trouble dealing with. He apparently wanted this all neatly tidied up so he could wash his hands of everything she'd brought to his door.

'That's what we all want, I guess.' Unfortunately, even if she had been at her ass-kicking, emotionally detached, sleeping-at-night best, this was going to be a monumental task. If by some miracle she could engage her father in conversation long enough to convince him of the plan, the practicalities alone would cripple her.

She needed help. She needed Nate. All that was left to do was swallow her pride and admit it.

'I know you can do this, Violet.' He had more faith in her than she had in herself. Or perhaps it was wishful thinking on his part, pre-empting the words that were going to come out of her mouth next.

'I don't think I can do this on my own. Will you help me?' She almost choked on the words that went against everything she'd strived for in adulthood. This was the second time in less than twenty-four hours she'd showed him her weakness.

By asking Nate to sleep with her, now begging him to bail her out, she made her new life into a sham. She'd flown back into town as a city slicker, an independent career woman who hadn't relied on anyone to help her make it in the Big Smoke. Now she was back to being that simpering, frightened girl she'd done her best to escape.

A wave of nausea crested over her as she waited for what seemed like an eternity. He'd turned down her request last night and she wouldn't blame him for doing the same again. He didn't owe her anything and he certainly didn't need this clingy, emotional side of her any more than she did. She'd simply hoped Nate would be the one person who wouldn't hold the past against her.

'I'm sorry. I shouldn't have asked. You've done so much for us already and I know you're busy—' She tried to back out of this with her last scrap of dignity intact.

His brow was furrowed in contemplation and she could almost see his refusal making its way from his brain to his lips. This smart idea had been right up there with asking the man she'd unceremoniously dumped years before to jump into bed with her.

She got to her feet and scouted out the nearest toilets so she could have a good blub in private. It was her own fault she didn't have a friend in him now when she'd run out on him when he'd needed her the most.

'Wait!' Nate shot out a hand and grabbed her by the wrist, pressing against her bracelet and temporarily branding her skin with her seahorse charm. It was a reminder of everything she'd thrown away and apparently could never get back.

It was too late. The old Nate wouldn't have hesitated to offer his support.

'Don't worry about it, Nate. I've dumped my problems on you once too often. I'll put in a few phone calls myself tomorrow—the bank, Citizens Advice, the Samaritans…' She forced a smile past the lump in her throat and her trembling bottom lip. Even though she'd been content on her own for a long time, somehow the thought of not having him by her side now made her feel more alone than ever.

CHAPTER FOUR

'I'LL HELP. WE'LL FIGURE this out together if that's what you want?' Nate hadn't known what he was going to say until the words were out of his mouth. He hadn't known he was going to reach for her until she'd tried to walk away. Now it was too late to take any of it back. His conscience had got the better of him again when it became clear how desperate she was for him to stick around. Once upon a time he'd been in that very position, wishing she'd stay with him at any cost. Just because he'd been left in the cold it didn't mean he should do the same to Violet. He would never intentionally hurt her when her family had done such a sterling job of that throughout her entire life.

He'd hesitated with good reason. The 'no' had danced on his tongue where he couldn't quite catch it. This was everything he'd sworn to stay away from— Violet, Strachmore, and a commitment to be there for someone for more than purely physical reasons. It might've been easier to draw that line if they had slept together. But he couldn't bear to see that dejected look on her face again if he rejected her a second time.

Violet bit her lip and nodded her head. From everything he'd heard over the years, she'd had her life all figured out without assistance from anyone. He knew she must've been out of options to turn to him for help after all this time apart. A huge step backward for her. Lord knew he wasn't in a hurry to go back to the Dark Ages either, where everything revolved around her father's will, but he had to consider the long-term benefits. One pride-swallowing favour could render him guilt-free for the rest of his days from everyone who might expect something from him in the future. This would be a one-off.

He resigned himself to whatever fate had in store for him next as punishment for not learning his lesson the first time around. If he approached this new relationship with Violet with the logical side of his brain instead of that useless emotional one, he might just come out of this with what was left of his heart in one piece.

'Okay, then. First things first, we'll need to pay off the most pressing bills before applying for any licences. We can't have them cutting off the electric, or, God forbid, your father's champagne-of-the-month subscription before he gets home.'

Another nod. She was going to have to move from the back seat and take over some of the driving duties if his involvement here was to remain short-lived. He was assisting her in her hour of need, not enabling her to ignore the problem.

'How do you want to proceed with this, Violet?'

She was going to have to make decisions for herself and not get too comfortable with him being around. Once his idea was up and running, so was he. He'd thought he'd found his 'Get out of Jail Free' card by coming up with this venture in the first place. A pair of storm-coloured eyes had been his undoing yet again.

Perhaps he could persuade her to start wearing sunglasses and prevent any further forced promises being made in a hypnotic trance.

Violet inhaled a deep breath as though she was girding herself for the challenge ahead. The first good sign she was in this with him. 'We should sit down and go through the paperwork together to see exactly what we're dealing with.'

It was the logical first step and the proactive approach he wanted to see from her. However, it also meant spending more time together. Inevitable, he supposed, and also the main reason he'd initially resisted volunteering for being her second in command. He'd already proved how weak-willed he was when it came to Violet, barely surviving the last test of his strength.

'If you have everything with you now we could go through it in my office. I have some time before my cardiac clinic.' His attempt to avoid a repeat of their previous one-to-one at Strachmore earned him a raised eyebrow and a grin.

'I understand why you don't trust me not to rip your clothes off if we're left alone for too long, but I'm afraid I don't carry my father's shame around in my handbag. We'll have to come up with an alternative venue. Somewhere with a glass partition, perhaps, to protect you from unwarranted advances? Or would you prefer I was immobilised and trussed up *à la* Hannibal Lecter?'

It was his turn to give the dirty looks. He was simply taking necessary security measures to make sure this remained a platonic meeting.

'Let's not make this weird, Nate. I'm sure even you've been knocked back on occasion without being made to feel like a sex fiend by the other party.'

She was right. By shying away from being alone with her he was turning this into a bigger deal than it should be. There'd been instances where he'd turned down advances from patients and colleagues alike and he'd carried on without giving it a second thought. He shouldn't treat this, treat Violet, any different from anyone else. That was what had got him into trouble thus far.

'I can't say I've ever encountered that particular problem myself…'

He hit the jackpot with that one—a *'tut'* and an eye-roll combo.

'Well, Mr Smooth, I defer to your superiority in these matters. What shall it be? My place, yours, or somewhere neutral? Say, Belfast City Hall? It's a bit of a drive but there'll be plenty of people around to keep you safe.' This snarky Violet put him more at ease than the meek version even if she was making him the butt of her jokes.

If he was honest, he'd seen enough of Strachmore this last couple of days to last him another lifetime. The city hall was tempting but that merely compounded the theory he didn't trust her, or himself, not to act inappropriately. That only left one other option.

'My place it is. I can swing by after my shift to pick you and the paperwork up. Maybe even grab some takeaway to eat while we work?' He was going on the theory that at least if they were at his house they'd be playing by his rules. There was no chance of any last-minute sleepovers and absolutely no reminders of their shared past. He would set the boundaries and time limits on tonight's escapade.

'That would be great. I'll pop in and say goodbye

to Dad and head back to get things organised.' The smile back on her face was because of him. Her peace of mind came at the price of his but at least those eyes had their sparkle back.

'And I've got a waiting room full of patients to attend. Unless there's any emergencies I should be away around seven p.m.' He made a move to get back to Outpatients, where he was confident in his decision-making process.

'Thanks, Nate.'

Why did every pat on the head from Violet seem like a reward and a step back at the same time?

Violet couldn't sit still. She'd changed, twice, carefully applied, then removed, her make-up, and cooked a lasagne. All so she wouldn't come across to Nate as though she was trying too hard. This wasn't a date, it was an intervention of sorts. Yet the butterflies in her stomach were the same ones she'd had when she'd waited for him to take her to their fake prom.

Sure, she'd swapped her baby pink swing dress for jeans and the grey hoodie she usually wore for jogging, but it was the same sense of excitement making her fidgety at the prospect of spending the evening with him.

Until yesterday she'd forgotten the effect he had on her. It was entirely possible her subconscious had locked those memories away with the bad ones, fearing they were equally damaging to her equilibrium. Her London-based liaisons held no element of surprise when she was the one calling the shots. Having the upper hand enabled her to bail when things got too serious. Just as she had done with Nate. That had been a bigger step for her than leaving home, but one that had also given her the courage to protect herself first and foremost in her following relationships.

Now she was back to hanging around this big house waiting for Nate to rescue her. Except this time he was whisking her from a mountain of debt instead of the school dance she'd been dreading and taking her to his place instead of the old boathouse.

That had been the night her feelings for him had begun to change. He'd dressed in his best shirt and tie to escort her to their alternative prom. To this day no one knew she'd ditched the fancy hotel venue her classmates had attended for an evening in the draughty wooden shack. She'd been more comfortable there, safer, than in a room full of her peers.

Sweet sixteen and never been kissed but in his strong arms as they'd danced to the mix tape he'd made specially, she'd thought about it. He'd been the only one who'd taken her pleas that she hadn't wanted to go to her prom seriously but still wanted to make the night special for her. He'd always known what was best for her and it would be easy to sit back and let him make those judgement calls for her now, but deep down she realised those days were long gone.

She'd seen it in his reluctance to get involved, felt it when she'd had to ask for help rather than have him pre-empt it. It was down to her that things had changed between them and she hadn't regretted that decision until she'd had to come back and face him. It had been easier not to miss that close relationship when she wasn't seeing him every day.

She covered the lasagne dish with aluminium foil and put the salad ingredients into a portable container.

This way she was simply bringing dinner to a friend's house, leaving no room for misunderstanding when Nate wasn't paying for the food they'd eat together.

She'd been listening for a car horn to sound his arrival and hadn't expected him to ring the doorbell. Neither had she expected to see him waiting on her doorstep. All he'd needed were the bouquet of flowers and box of chocolates accessories and she'd found her dream date.

Not a date. Crisis management.

If she kept telling herself that they might both come out of this unscathed.

'Hey.' He scuffed his shoes on the stone steps the way he always had when they were kids, eager to get away from here as soon as she was ready before her father spotted him.

'Hey. I've just got to grab a few things and I'll meet you at the car.' She knew he was only standing here out of courtesy, being the gentleman her father had always told her she'd deserved.

After a quick dash inside to collect the makings of dinner, she joined him in the car.

'What's that?' He sniffed the air and peered at the mini tower of food containers on her knee as if she were using his vehicle to transfer toxic waste across the country.

'Dinner. Lasagne, to be more precise. I can't take credit for the salad but I made everything else from scratch.'

The car swerved as Nate turned to stare at her. 'Since when could you make more than burnt toast?'

Violet reached across to straighten the steering wheel so he didn't run them off the road. That split second of closeness made her heart beat a little faster. His breath was hot on the back of her neck, his frame strong around her and his spicy aftershave so enticing she wanted to sink back into him. She didn't.

'I know it was our secret snack of choice in the days of sneaking into the kitchen but the single life called for something more exciting and nutritious. The lack of a social life gives me plenty of time to experiment in the kitchen after work.' She was rambling now but since she was practically sprawled in his lap things could get awkward quickly if they let silence descend.

'I…er…think we're good now.' He gave her the nod to extricate herself from his side of the car.

Their brief encounter had given her more than a warm feeling inside. A tingling sensation had started at the top of her thighs and was steadily making its way south. It took a few seconds staring at the up-turned dish in her lap before she made the connection.

'Ack!' The bottom of her sweatshirt and her jeans were now coated in a hot tomato and minced beef marinade. Thankfully the pasta layers had remained intact between the foil and the dish so she was able to rescue it with a quick flip.

'What's wrong?'

'I spilled dinner. Don't worry, I caught most of it.' In her lap, which was now stinging beneath her denims. She tried not to make a scene and draw even more attention to her stupidity.

Hs curiosity deepened his forehead into a frown when he cast a glance in her direction. 'Are you all right?'

'Fine,' she said through gritted teeth as molten lasagne lava singed her flesh.

'We're here now anyway. I'll take a look once we're inside.'

They pulled up outside a very modern, very secluded two-storey glass building overlooking Dundrum Bay. Nothing like the city-based apartment she'd pictured him in.

'I had no idea you lived so close.' Even more surprising than this sophisticated bachelor pad with only the local wildlife for company was the fact Strachmore was merely a ten-minute drive away.

'Only for this last couple of years. I've worked all over Ireland but when the position opened up in Silent Valley, I decided to move back. It turned out I missed the peace and quiet out here. And it's still far enough away to deter my parents from dropping in when they feel like it.'

Violet imagined no one got beyond the gates without some sort of personal invitation. She tried not to think about those who had passed through here and took comfort in the fact she'd been personally chauffeured door-to-door by the owner.

Nate climbed out of the driver seat and walked around to her side of the car. He opened the door and took possession of their dinner remains in one hand. Even as he helped her out with his free hand, it was obvious he was assessing the extent of her injuries.

Violet groaned as the cool air made contact and increased her discomfort.

'That's it. Get inside and take your clothes off.' Nate opened the front door and practically shoved her inside.

'I bet you say that to all the ladies,' Violet snarked with a grimace.

In a different situation that line would've got her

hot and bothered for other reasons. Now she was simply cringing at the turn this night had taken already. It wasn't the civilised evening she'd planned.

'Only the ones who turn up on my doorstep with third-degree burns.' He chivvied her upstairs to the bathroom while he carried the source of tonight's humiliation to the kitchen.

Violet eased her jeans down to reveal angry red welts across her thighs. They were throbbing so badly now as she sat on the edge of the bath she wasn't sure how she'd ever put her clothes back on again.

She took a towel from the rail and ran it under the tap before draping it across her sensitive skin. The relief was only temporary as the heat from her burns began again in earnest.

There was a knock on the door. 'Violet? Are you okay in there?'

She wondered how it had come to sitting in her underwear in Nate's bathroom nursing a lasagne scalding.

'Umm…have you got any antiseptic cream I can use?' With any luck a dollop of cold cream and a few glasses of wine would help her forget this had ever happened.

'In the bathroom cabinet but I think I should take a look first. Can I come in?'

Her mortification was complete as Nate joined her, fully dressed, in the confined space.

'May I?' He hunkered down in front of her asking permission to see her mishap for himself.

She slowly lifted away the towel covering the last of her dignity. In keeping with her not-a-date mantra she'd forgone all sexy, lacy underwear in favour of the comfy cartoon knickers one of her friends had given her for Christmas. Her cheeks burned as much as her thighs.

'Ouch. It looks painful but you'll live. It mightn't feel like it now but it's pretty superficial. You won't require hospital treatment, although you should really keep those burns under running water for a few minutes.' He reached for the shower attachment over the bath and turned the tap on.

As Violet swung around to put her bare legs into the bath she was grateful he hadn't made her strip and get into his fancy-pants shower cubicle in the corner with more nozzles and buttons than she'd know what to do with.

Nate rolled his sleeves up as he administered the cooling jets of water to the burn site. After a few minutes of relative silence her teeth began to chatter from the cold.

'I think that should do for now.' He patted her dry with another towel then retrieved a tub of cream from the bathroom cabinet.

There was such a calm, gentle manner about him Violet could see what made him a great doctor. He applied the cream in soothing strokes, not batting an eyelid at her choice of underwear. It was unnerving having him so close, paying such attention to delicate parts of her. He was tender and considerate, and Violet was forced to clamp down on inappropriate thoughts as arousal took hold of her.

Nate was still intent on treating her burn, apparently oblivious to the erotic nature his touch had taken on in her corrupted mind. If his strong fingers massaged any further up her thigh she might spontaneously combust. And probably not very quietly.

As if reading her thoughts. Nate withdrew and got to his feet. 'We'll get you some painkillers but you should be fine. I wouldn't try and get your jeans on again though—they'll rub too much against the skin.'

'I'm not prancing around your house all night in my undies. Imagine the gossip.'

Nate looked as horrified by that suggestion as she was. Clearly all that electricity had been surging in one direction only.

Nate was having difficulty putting out of his mind that image of Violet wandering through his house in the altogether, not least because she was already half-naked in front of him. 'I'll go see if I can find you something to wear and throw those clothes in the washing machine before they stain.'

He needed space, and a reality check. Violet might not be his patient per se, but he definitely shouldn't be thinking about the softness of her skin while he was treating her. Not even her novelty underwear was helping to rein in his wayward libido. It reminded him he was one of the few who'd ever seen that fun side of her. A reminder there was more to her than glamour and pain.

He retreated to the sanctuary of his bedroom where there was nothing to stimulate his Violet fantasies any further. Except the huge bed with the black leather headboard dominating the room. He turned his back on his pride and joy and yanked the wardrobe open. He'd known nothing in here would ever fit her but he'd taken the time out to compose himself before more than his trousers became uncomfortable.

The rows of dry-cleaned shirts and trousers were

practical for a busy doctor but not much use for a slender burn victim who needed covering for both of their sakes. He paused flicking through the rails when he came to his lab coats and scrubs but apparently even they were too much for his over-sexed imagination to handle. He snatched a white shirt from the hanger. The sooner he covered her up, the sooner they could carry on with the real reason she was in his house.

It took a few seconds for his befuddled brain to clear so he could remember what that was.

She was still perched on the end of his bath where he'd left her, looking for all the world as if she were in that post-coital, comfortable-wearing-nothing stage. Except he hadn't had that pleasure and nothing about this was comfortable for him.

'Here. This should be long enough to wear as a dress with the bonus of letting the air around those burns.' He practically threw the shirt at her in his haste to get away. He even contemplated going back to the en-suite in his bedroom for his own cold shower.

When his stomach began to rumble it gave him a different body part to focus on. 'Just throw your clothes in the laundry and I'll see if I can rescue what's left of dinner.'

He reconstructed the layers of pasta as best he could and plated it up with the well-tossed salad. Violet re-appeared in the doorway as he was setting it out on the dining table and diverted his appetite elsewhere.

The shirt skimmed the tops of her thighs, covering her curves and brightly coloured underwear, but it did nothing to hide those long, toned legs. He'd never be able to wear that shirt again without seeing her in it or smelling her sweet perfume.

He sat down at the table and took a long drink of water, trying to drown that persistent idea that this was how she'd look the next morning if she'd spent the night. All that could save him now was that folder of truth spelling out in great detail why he shouldn't get involved with the sexy heiress. She came with more than just overnight baggage.

Violet could see it written all over Nate's face that he wanted this night to be over. They ate dinner in virtual silence although she suspected neither of them had much of an appetite. Despite her efforts to make this a casual arrangement it had all the hallmarks of an awkward first date, or a really bad seduction attempt. After her last botched come-on, it wouldn't be beyond the realms of possibility for one to accuse her of faking a lasagne-related injury so she had an excuse to strip. If only she'd planned this. Or, Nate had been interested in her half-naked body.

'That was delicious. My compliments to the chef.' He cleared away the dishes in his obvious hurry to get down to the real business of the evening and send her on her way before she caused any more embarrassment.

'Thank you, and mine to the doctor.' Although she was still in some discomfort, the pain had considerably subsided, with only the occasional flare-up of mortification.

She hoped she'd recover sufficiently to put her own clothes back on, dirty or not. She didn't fancy doing the walk of shame home in Nate's shirt under false pretences. That was normally only a liberty taken after spending a night together. Naked.

'Let's see what the damage is.' He'd retrieved the folder of paperwork she'd left in the car so they were able to finally get the evening back on track and prevent her from forming any more ideas of how she could get him into bed.

Violet spread the bills and threatening letters over the table, glad she had him beside her to help get her through this.

'We've got household bills, unpaid credit cards, bank statements…'

They sorted the final demands into easier-to-handle piles. Her father would be apoplectic if he suspected they were going through his personal things but this was for his own good as well as hers. Perhaps one day he'd realise that.

'I'm sure some of these companies might be sympathetic and suspend payment for a while if you contact them and explain your father's current circumstances. I don't think they would deal with me since I'm not family.'

'I'll phone around first thing. It's worth a try.' It would help her if they could find some way to stagger the payments so she could work her way through these gradually.

Nate frowned as he gathered a handful of scarlet bills. 'Unfortunately, there are quite a few of these which require immediate payment before you find yourself cut off from civilisation.'

Electricity, telephone and rates bills were ones she couldn't afford to ignore even if her father had.

'And the credit cards are going to need at least minimum payment made on them. Not to mention the loans he's taken out with sky-high interest rates.' It took every scrap of courage inside her not to rip everything up and pretend she'd never seen it. Instead, she created a new 'red alert' pile to be dealt with in the morning.

'There's definitely no emergency fund anywhere to buy some time?' Nate's optimism had long outlived hers.

A thorough read of the bank statements confirmed her father had been living on a wing and a prayer for quite some time. No doubt his good name had given him more leeway than most but little else.

'I'm afraid his finances are as dire as my own.'

'Can I help?' Nate reached for the nightmare she was holding in her hand but she snatched it away from his grasp.

'No!' She'd put upon him enough, let him pry further into the family secrets than anyone, but she had to draw the line somewhere. Asking Nate for financial assistance would be the final insult to all involved. Her father would never forgive her and she didn't want Nate to feel even more used than he already did. If she could find any other way to bail out Strachmore than borrowing from him she would.

'It's only money, Violet. Something I can help with.'

It's only money.

How many times had she heard those words from her father? Enough to know it was never *'only money'.* It annoyed her more hearing it from someone who'd worked hard to make his fortune, not inherited and squandered it. It was more than money, it was a matter of pride.

'Thanks but I don't want to go down that road. I can cover a few of the smaller debts for now and I have an idea of how to raise the rest.' She didn't have much in the way of inheritance other than headaches and a useless title but there were a few things she could sell that her father had absolutely no say in.

'I don't like the sound of that.'

He had his arms folded across his chest, his pride probably wounded by her refusal of help, but Violet hadn't relinquished total control just yet. Nate was her support but it was important she didn't compromise her own principles to suit him. Otherwise, that made a mockery of everything she'd railed so hard against. She might as well be married in that case.

'Thanks to my mother I'm still a woman of certain means.'

'You can't—'

'I'm going to sell her necklace. It's only jewellery after all.' Suddenly the ball was firmly back in her court.

'I won't let you do that.' Nate couldn't stand back and watch her throw away the only thing of worth left from her mother. Not on behalf of someone who didn't appreciate her and certainly not when there was an alternative on offer.

Money he had, could give her easier than anything else when it held no emotional attachment for him. It could solve the problem and let him off the hook a hell of a lot quicker if she'd accept it.

'You won't *let* me? Who the hell do you think you are telling me what I can and can't do?' Violet leaned across the table to blast him as she battled for control. With that passion she could've been the CEO of her own company, defending her assets in the boardroom.

Assets he was getting a good view of every time she leaned over.

'Your friend. I know how much your mother's things mean to you.' He walked around the table beside her so this supposed *friend* wasn't getting excited with every glimpse of her white cotton bra.

'I have some of her other belongings, which don't represent the problems that kept her awake at night. Expensive jewellery was Dad's way of showing off money he didn't have, not an expression of love for my mother.' She had that defiant tilt to her chin she used to have when she was challenging her parents' authority.

Nate didn't want her to think she didn't have anyone in her corner. He was there, yelling advice from behind the ropes.

'I don't want you to give up something you love just to make a point to your father. You might come to regret it.'

'Been there, done that.' She was talking about him. He could see it in that wistful smile and he wanted to believe she'd loved him once. It meant everything to him to know she might've regretted leaving him. That he hadn't imagined the strength of their bond and he'd been more than part of the fixtures at Strachmore.

All of the anger he'd been holding against her for these past years seemed to fade and render his resistance to touching her futile. He reached out to tuck a wayward strand of hair behind her ear.

'How did we end up here, Vi?'

Things could've worked out so differently if she'd been brave then and given them a chance regardless of what anyone thought. He'd been so in love with her all she'd had to do was give him the word and he would've gone anywhere with her, done anything for her. Now he was a man on his own, too scarred to let anyone into his life.

'I don't know but sometimes I wish I could go back.'

With Violet standing here in his dining room wearing nothing more than his shirt and a smile, this was as far from those innocent days as they got. 'I can't say I'd rather be anywhere else.'

He leaned in to kiss her, reasoning twice in twelve years wasn't going to wreak too much havoc. He simply wanted to find out if her lips were as soft and sweet as he remembered. They were.

He should've left it at one gentle peck on the lips, enough to reconnect and erase the bad feeling left with her departure. When he opened his eyes and saw her lips parted for more, felt her hands slide around his neck in submission, he couldn't recall any reason to hold back. They both wanted this. In some ways they needed it to enable them to finally move on.

He slipped his arms around her waist and pulled her closer to deepen the kiss he'd waited too long to repeat. As Violet pressed her body against his it soon became clear this was more than one innocent smooch. His erection grew ever stronger with every flick of her tongue against his, every breathy moan of acceptance.

With his hands at her waist he lifted her off the floor and set her on the edge of the table. Violet gave a yelp against his mouth in surprise but wrapped her legs around him to keep him in place. With one sweep of his arm he cleared the papers from the table to the floor so he could lay her down. He went with her, kissing the exposed skin at the open V of his shirt. She was a feast he intended to enjoy guilt-free.

Violet's limbs had turned to jelly with that first

brush of his lips on hers and made her forget they were in the middle of an argument. Her thoughts were hazy with desire but she'd known he'd only been trying to help as always. She'd been the one to let emotions get in the way by almost letting slip the extent of her feelings for him in the past and lighting the touch paper for this chemistry that had been bubbling between them since she'd come home. If she was honest it had always been there and it had been a long, hard fight to keep it at bay, and not always a successful one.

That second kiss had nothing to do with the past. This time around they were acting on pure carnal instinct. Having sex on a dining table was as animalistic and far from emotional entanglement as she could hope for.

As if to illustrate her point, Nate was reaching beneath her shirt to remove her panties and making her wet with want for him. Her skin was so sensitive every brush of his fingers sent a shudder rippling through her in anticipation. She couldn't distinguish her scald marks from the rest of her skin burning up with his every touch.

He stepped back and tossed her underwear over his shoulder with a grin, leaving Violet squirming on the hard wood surface. She didn't care how uncomfortable this was, all that mattered was the ache he'd created inside her and how soon he was going to cure it.

Not any time soon, it seemed, as he began a torturously slow ascent along her thigh using his mouth and tongue. Her body was on high alert—her nipples hardening, her arousal heading to meet him—as he teased her with a sample of everything he could do for her. To her.

Violet braced her hands on the table, fighting off the too early waves of ecstasy trying to drag her into oblivion. She wanted this to last as long as humanly possible because in all likelihood it could be their first and last surrender to temptation.

Somewhere in the distance she heard a faint buzzing sound. She hadn't figured Nate to be into anything kinky but, spread-eagled before him, it wouldn't be right to start getting prudish now. She heard Nate groan and bit back one of her own. He was certainly taking his time. If he was into that tantric nonsense she was going to have to take matters into her own hands pretty soon.

'I'm really sorry, Violet.' The sound of his voice and the cold air hitting her where his hot lips had once been pulled her sharply back from the brink.

'Hmm?' She was struggling to sit up, her body limp with desire and Nate-tending.

'I have to go. I'm needed at the hospital.' He waved a battery-powered device at her, which was unfortunately ending their evening, not getting it off to an exciting start.

'You've been paged?' She came close to banging her head on the table in frustration.

''Fraid so.' The bulge in his trousers and his sad eyes said he was as disappointed as she was that this was over before it had begun.

Violet scrabbled to sit up, her hands sliding on the remnants of the bills scattered around. Her guilt receptors kicked in immediately. Putting her own needs first had saved her sanity in the past, but in this case she'd lost sight of what was most important. They were supposed to be working on helping her father, taking steps to make sure she could escape at the end of all of this. Getting jiggy with Nate certainly wasn't doing anything to fast-track those plans.

He was integral to all aspects of her life here and she didn't want to jeopardise any of that. She should be doing everything she could to try and get her father back in his rightful place instead of finding reasons to keep her around.

'It's probably for the best. You're my dad's cardiologist…you're helping me with Strachmore…that has to be more important than this…us.'

Nate was left breathless with the full impact of Violet's comment. It was bad enough that he'd been physically pained at having to call a halt to this moment of madness but Violet's reaction had body-slammed him and stolen what was left of those feel-good endorphins.

He was acceptable in his professional capacity treating her father, helpful in his role as financial advisor, but, when she'd stopped to think about it, not good enough even as a temporary bed partner.

Of course, hooking up with Violet hadn't been a good idea; he'd known that from the first time they'd almost done this. He'd simply got carried away with the revelation she might've loved him at some point. If he'd been thinking with his head he might've realised that had made her even more callous for leaving him.

'I have to go straight into surgery so I'm afraid I won't have time to take you home. I'll leave money for a taxi. Make sure you lock the door on your way out.' This time he wasn't going to sit around brooding about why she didn't want him. He had a job and a life outside Lady Dempsey's whim.

CHAPTER FIVE

VIOLET HAD KEPT herself as busy as possible in the days following Lasagne-Gate. She'd managed to sell her mother's diamond necklace back to the jewellers her father had originally bought it from, for probably a fraction of what he'd paid for it, but it had eased some of the financial burden heaped on her shoulders. For the best part of forty-eight hours she'd had the phone attached to her ear, fending off the bailiffs before they descended on the castle to seize the family silver. It had taken a lot of time, talking and money but she'd managed to pacify most of the creditors chasing her father. For now. Unfortunately none of it had managed to keep Nate from her thoughts for long.

If the hospital hadn't paged him she had no doubt they would've rocked that dining table all night long. That call had given her the clarity to remember how much sleeping together could complicate things. Even he seemed to have had a change of heart since then, reverting to that aloof Nate she'd encountered on that first night. There'd been no mention of the fact they'd almost done the deed at his house, neither had there been an invitation to finish what they'd started. It was a shame her body wouldn't let her forget the sizzling after-dinner entertainment.

She and Nate had kept interaction about Strachmore matters in strictly public areas since that night but it didn't prevent her from thinking about what they'd done in private. His talk of fire-risk assessments could have well been about the physical effect he had on her. A five-minute chat these days was enough to leave her hot and bothered when she could still feel his lips inching along her inner thigh. It wasn't fair only one of them appeared to be suffering, and it was confidence-crushing to find he had no lingering desire to see that night to a conclusion. Even if her conscience had played a part in bringing matters to an end.

Unresolved sexual tension aside, this past couple of nights had been tough. It didn't cost her a second thought to come home every night to her London flat but Strachmore seemed to amplify her loneliness. The chimes of antique clocks echoing through the empty house taunted her, reminded her of the time that had passed between her and everyone here. She couldn't get it back and some day her lone occupancy of the castle would be permanent.

When she was with Nate there wasn't a moment to dwell on the past, or the future. With him, it was all about the present. She missed his company at night, especially when she had absolutely nothing to come home to. He was part of the reason she was spending longer at the hospital. It certainly wasn't all about being in her father's presence. She was as sympathetic as anyone could be for everything he'd gone through but his self-pity was exhausting.

He was still in some pain and Violet knew a lot of

his bad temper was down to fear and frustration. It didn't make it any easier for her to come here two or three times a day and bear the brunt of his complaints. Especially when she was working so hard behind the scenes to make his life as uncomplicated as possible when he got home. That revelation was another headache waiting to happen. She knew he would explode when he found out and she would have to justify the fact she'd cared enough to try and alleviate some of his stress. Samuel Dempsey never asked for help and he certainly wouldn't appreciate it.

Even now Violet could see a commotion around him at the nurses' station. Over the past couple of days he'd progressed to bathing on his own and taking short walks around the room. She suspected they'd come to rue their encouragement of his mobility. Now they'd all be in the line of fire.

'Dad? Is everything okay?'

She fought the urge to turn on her heel and let someone else deal with him. That selfish attitude was probably part of the reason Strachmore was in the mess it was. She'd had to put herself first at eighteen but that meant the Earl and his bloody-mindedness had been left unchecked for too long. He hadn't been accountable to anyone in her absence and it was a big ask to expect him to take on any advice now. They were both going to have to shoulder some responsibility for the current state of affairs and take steps to rectify the damage. As much as she longed to have this all neatly wrapped up so she could get back to her own life, Violet wasn't convinced she was strong enough to make a difference.

'I'm fed up with being poked and prodded every day

in this…this torture chamber. How am I supposed to rest when I'm woken every five minutes for scans and tests? There's absolutely no respect for me here and I've had enough. I want to go home.' He slammed his fist down on the desk and Violet jumped, along with several of the nurses.

If her prayers were answered she'd disappear into the bowels of the earth any second now and not have to face these people as her father spat abuse at them. It was different when she was the one subjected to his tirades—she was family, had grown up listening to them—but these people should be exempt.

'The doctors and nurses have worked tirelessly to get you well again. You've got to understand these tests are necessary—they're not done out of spite.' Sometimes it was like talking to a petulant child when she tried to reason with him. When he was in one of his rages there was no logic involved, only emotion. The overriding one usually being anger. In these circumstances it was liable to kill him.

'I was explaining to your father that we want to move him onto a main ward to continue his recovery. We would prefer to continue the ECG monitoring for a few more days there before he goes home.'

She hadn't seen Nate standing in the melee until her father had turned to glare at her impudence. But there he was, standing toe to toe with him and trying to run interference for her. Even when he seemed to be avoiding her his chivalry still shone through.

'Do you know who I am?'

Violet cringed as he played the nobility card. The one that had done nothing but bring her embarrassment over the years.

'Yes, Lord Dempsey, and I assure you you'll receive the same standard of treatment as all of our patients.' Social status had never held any sway with Nate either. It wouldn't need to, given his professional approach to his work. Violet was certain every one of his patients was treated with the utmost respect no matter what their background, perhaps even despite it in cases such as this.

'That's what I'm afraid of. Thanks but no, thanks. I want to go home to a clean bed where the staff are paid more than the minimum wage to take care of me.'

'Dad! That's completely out of order.' Not to mention factually incorrect. It showed how delusional her father was when he was under the impression his staff were being paid more than a qualified cardiologist.

'I appreciate this is a difficult time for you but we need to take precautions for the good of your own health. Your physical activity needs to be increased gradually and we would like to make sure you attend cardiac rehabilitation.'

It could've been another run-in between the pair when Nate was nothing more than a schoolboy, given the manner in which her father continued to speak to him. Not once had Nate been forced to raise his voice to make his point even though he was surely wounded by the insults flying around. Violet had never seen anyone stand their ground with the Earl in full flow. Even when she'd mounted her great rebellion she'd done it over the telephone rather than face to face.

'I'm sure those are matters which my own doctor can facilitate. He's a man with over forty years of experience. I trust *him*.' Another dig at Nate, both personally and professionally.

Not that her father would've taken any more notice of a different staff member, Violet was sure, but this continual slight against Nate was very hard even for her to stomach. By denying his achievements he somehow rendered her own unremarkable. The great Earl would never admit he'd been wrong in trying to force them into their society pigeonholes or congratulate them on their successes. Until now Violet hadn't realised she'd been waiting for his approval.

Nate had dealt with his fair share of obstinate patients over the years. People had different coping mechanisms when it came to facing their own mortality and sometimes that manifested itself against the very staff treating them. Usually he took it in his stride. After all, who was to say he wouldn't lash out if he were the one on the other end of the stethoscope? Today he was finding new limits to his tolerance he didn't know he was capable of.

In the space of ten minutes his integrity and his professionalism had been called into question by someone who'd known him since he'd been a child. That was the problem, he supposed. His parents' employer was still judging him on the nonconforming teen he imagined had robbed him of his daughter. It was ironic that Nate hadn't gained anything from that loss except the successful career that was now being maligned. Regardless of how hard he tried, those from Strachmore would never see him as anything but the next generation of domestic staff. The only difference was the Dempseys weren't paying him to take this abuse.

He'd even had to battle his own family to pursue his chosen career. In their eyes by going to medical school he'd thrown away the honour of working for the aristocracy. As if their allegiance meant he should've sacrificed his prospects too. They hadn't understood his resistance to doing manual labour so a privileged family could sit comfortably on their pedestals. There'd been no support, financially or otherwise, as they'd seen him as some sort of traitor.

That attitude had created a distance between Nate and his parents. He'd hated them at times for their blind devotion to the Earl when they'd effectively disowned their own son for the sin of ambition. In a roundabout way they had been part of his success when his anger had driven him to reach the pinnacle of his career. These days he accepted them for who they were in the hope they would some day do the same for him. He'd learned it wasn't healthy to hold on to grudges or look for answers where there was none, and taken back control of his life by simply accepting circumstances beyond his control. No matter how much it jarred.

'In that case all I can do is ask you to wait until we have your discharge papers ready. We need to have it in writing that you are going against our recommendations by leaving before your treatment here is complete. There's also the matter of arranging your medication before you leave.' If it was merely a case of one stubborn patient showing he was still in control of his own fate, Nate would sign off and move on to the next patient who actually wanted his help. That was practically impossible when Violet was standing opposite worrying her bottom lip with her teeth.

'I will not linger here a second longer than is absolutely necessary.' The Earl continued to bluster, his cheeks reddening as he pointed a knobbly finger at

Nate as though he were holding him to ransom. It was the other way around. As tempted as Nate was to have Security bundle him out of the door, he couldn't bear to be responsible for anything happening to Violet's only surviving family member.

'That's entirely your prerogative, but it would be in your best interests to wait for the reasons I've stated. I would also ask you would do so quietly to prevent any further disruption to your fellow patients on the ward.'

His thoughts were also for Violet, who was standing with her arms wrapped around her waist in a self-comforting gesture being completely blanked by her father. The more distressed he could see her becoming, the harder it was for Nate to keep his own temper in check.

'How dare—?'

'Dad! He said he'll sort it. Go and lie down before you do yourself any more damage.' Violet cut him off as he launched into another rant, her hands now planted on her hips.

The strength of her bravery was belied by her trembling bottom lip, which only Nate seemed to notice. The Earl, whether exhausted by his own ire or his daughter's, finally returned to his bed with a grumble.

Violet visibly relaxed when the argument was brought to a close. Nate had never been privy to the rows she must've witnessed at Strachmore and, although he'd been dismayed at times by his own parents' behaviour, he'd never been afraid in his own home. He had seen the fear in her eyes as she'd confronted her father about his attitude and Nate had just witnessed how vile this man could be. Although he'd tried to back off before he and Violet acted out any more erotic scenes on his furniture, he couldn't seem to stay away.

If he'd truly meant to keep his distance he could've transferred Samuel Dempsey's care elsewhere and reduced the chances of running into his daughter, but Nate was very much a part of this dysfunctional relationship. Despite the constant reminders he would never be a suitable match for Violet, it had been hell trying to put that night at his place out of his mind. The handprints left on his table were a frustrating reminder they were physically compatible, combustible even, if not couple material.

Now today's drama was over they were left staring at each other pretending there wasn't a conflict of interests going on. He had history with Violet, and her father, which he was doing his best not to let cloud his judgement. Unfortunately whatever happened with this patient was always going to affect his personal life too.

'You can't let him leave.' Violet was imploring him to intervene with those big expressive eyes. He preferred the dark glittering sapphires when she was in the throes of passion to the all too familiar worried baby blues.

'Now *you're* trying to tell *me* what's for the best?'

She'd almost bitten his head off for daring to do the same over the matter of her mother's jewellery. A matter that he still wasn't happy to lay to rest.

'I'm serious, Nate. You said yourself he should stay here. He's not ready to go home.' Everything in her tense body language said she wasn't ready for it either. If he could've chained her father to the bed rather than subject her to any more of his outbursts, he would've found a way to do it. They both knew her father's return to Strachmore would throw everything they'd been working towards into chaos.

'My hands are tied, I'm afraid. He's an adult, of, allegedly, sound mind. I can only advise him to remain under my care, not force him. This is clearly also an extremely volatile environment for him and staying won't benefit him or the other patients around him.' He hated himself for doing this to her. While she was doing her best to be strong, Nate had seen enough of her telltale signs to see she was struggling.

'What am I going to do with him? I'm a mental-health nurse, I'm not qualified for cardiac care.' Violet kept glancing across to his bed, where he was still grumbling and slamming his things around. It was impossible to tell which of them was more stressed here.

'I'll get in touch with his GP, see if he can't persuade him to stay where he is. Failing that, between me, you and my parents, we'll have to muddle through.' Another commitment he'd made just so he could put that smile back on Violet's face. There was also that niggle about not being able to perform the angioplasty making him uneasy. It was the first time he'd been unable to complete his duty of care to the full.

'You'll come and check on him?'

'We'll probably have to find some covert way of doing it but I won't let you take this on alone.' At least then he could keep an eye on the Earl's recovery and watch for any complications arising from his refusal of conventional treatment.

'You won't *let* me, huh?'

'Well, I thought on this occasion you might concede a small piece of that iron will.'

They exchanged wry smiles over the private joke. The origin of which was rooted in that night at his house. Not long after they'd argued over Violet's stance on selling her mother's jewellery, they'd ended up locking tongues, and almost a lot more besides, on his dining room table.

He began to regret his decision to wear a tie today as the air seemed to dissipate and leave him struggling to breathe. It made no difference if they were alone or in a ward full of people when it came to chemistry. Violet was staring at his lips and he could tell she was recalling the last time she'd yielded to him.

The silence that fell between them crackled with tension and unfinished business. It didn't matter to his libido that both members of the Dempsey family had judged him and found him wanting. He was programmed to enjoy the benefits of a physical relationship without any emotional messiness and he shouldn't start changing the rules now. It was his pride keeping him awake at night imagining what could've been instead of living it.

'Dr Taylor, you're needed in Room One.'

Nate was reminded he was supposed to be working, not trying to figure out a way he could sleep with Violet without compromising his principles. He gave the nurse a nod of acknowledgement.

'I'd best get on and do what I'm paid for. Don't worry, Violet, I'll make sure your father has the best care whether it's here or at home.' The promises tripped off his tongue as easy as denial and insults flowed from Samuel Dempsey's. They were both trapped in a pattern of self-destructive behaviour that could jeopardise their future if they weren't careful. Sooner or later they were going to have to make changes in order to survive. For Nate that would entail cutting out more than whiskey and cigars.

True to his word Nate had sent in a crack team of physiotherapists and dieticians to speak to the Earl. Neither Violet nor the forest's worth of advice leaflets had been enough to convince him to stay put. As usual, they'd all had to bend to his will and accept he was going home. He'd offended so many people along the way, there was a certain amount of relief mixed with Violet's trepidation.

Regardless of their lengthy estrangement she still felt the need to apologise to everyone he came into contact with for his abrupt manner. She should have been firmer with him, tried harder to make him modify his behaviour, but the truth was she was still intimidated by him herself. If he objected to her interference and really cut loose on her, she wasn't sure she would turn out to be any stronger than her mother.

She'd given up any right to tell him what to do when she'd left home at eighteen and vice versa. There was no way she would've accepted him swanning back into her life and trying to run it for her after all this time either. The difference was, she wasn't putting other people's livelihoods in jeopardy with a blinkered approach to her finances. She'd made damn sure she had no dependants for that very reason, when it had cost her so much to simply take responsibility for herself.

It was late afternoon before they were ready to leave, much to her father's continued agitation. He didn't seem to grasp the fact that a crotchety old man going against medical advice wasn't the top priority on a ward full of seriously ill patients.

Not even the whistling porter who came to escort him from CCU escaped his wrath.

'I'm not a cripple,' he said and kicked the wheel of the wheelchair in disgust.

'It's only to take you to the door, Dad. Bill's picking us up outside. The physio said gentle exercise only, remember? You don't want to end up exhausted before you leave the grounds.' She imagined by this stage they were all glad to see the back of him from the department.

He was already out of breath with the effort it had taken to get dressed but he eventually got into the chair with a huff.

'A lot of fuss about nothing, if you ask me.'

She hadn't asked him, because that had the potential for her to lose her temper and demand to know why it was impossible for him to thank Nate for saving his life. They might get into hostile territory sooner than anticipated and run the risk of shattering the fragile remains of their father-daughter relationship, dooming Strachmore for ever.

As they made their way through the corridors she hoped to catch a glimpse of Nate, but he undoubtedly had his hands full with clinics and surgery. His skill in his field still astounded her, and she appreciated the time he'd dedicated to helping her even if her father didn't. He'd borne the brunt of her parent's rudeness through no fault of his own.

She wondered how much of that bitterness was actually apportioned to her. Her father had always associated her belligerent attitude with Nate's influence rather than his own tyranny. There was the possibility he blamed him for encouraging her to break out on her own. In which case she was going to have to set the record straight with a few home truths.

She'd never stopped to consider how her new start in London might have impacted on those she'd left behind. It had been easier to believe they'd all carried on as normal instead of adding more ballast to her burden of guilt. Only now were the consequences of her actions, her cowardice, becoming clear.

The next step was for all those who'd messed up to hold their hands up and admit their mistakes so they could start to move on from past transgressions. Even Nate, who appeared to have his life together, hadn't managed to let go of all responsibility to Strachmore. She owed it to him to enable that final break but just not yet. She had an inkling she was going to need his support more than ever now she was faced with living under her father's rule once more.

The Taylors did enough fussing over her father to enable her to take a back seat for a short while. When they were fawning over him his level of churlishness significantly decreased and gave Violet a reprieve from her 'tightly coiled spring' act every time he opened his mouth.

Bill had kindly arranged for his bed to be moved down to the ground floor to save him from having to take the stairs and Margaret had prepared a light dinner following his new dietary regime. It was only when the couple went home that the interminable silence fell at the dining table.

Of course he'd refused to take a dinner tray on his

lap, insisted on keeping things 'normal' with the formal dining, regardless of how ludicrous it was with only the two of them seated around the massive mahogany table. She suspected this charade was more for his benefit than hers. He looked like the king of his castle perched at the head of the table even if he mightn't feel it.

'I've missed Mrs Taylor's cooking,' she said to break the tense atmosphere spoiling her appetite.

'There was nothing stopping you coming back if you missed it that much.' He didn't miss a beat as he scored a point against her in between spoonfuls of soup.

There was nothing to be gained by getting into a fight now, when he was still wearing a hospital band around his wrist. They could get into the whys and wherefores of their non-relationship when he was fully recovered and she wasn't afraid of causing him to relapse.

'I've been so busy with work I haven't had much time for holidays.' It wasn't completely untrue. She'd simply omitted to tell him he was the reason she didn't take any.

'For twelve years?' He paused mid-slurp to raise a bushy white eyebrow.

She'd never been a particularly good liar.

'I didn't think I'd be very welcome.' She wasn't even sure she was now. At the minute his attitude towards her labelled her as more of an uninvited guest rather than the prodigal daughter returned to the loving arms of her father.

'I never asked you to leave in the first place.'

This was exactly the sort of backwards-and-forwards blame game she'd hoped to avoid.

'Well, I'm here now. I have some time off to take while you recuperate.' The way her nerves were stretched she might very well need some extra time to recover herself when this was all over.

'Why the sudden interest in me now? Or did you only come back to claim your inheritance? I'm sorry if I ruined your plans but it seems I'm going to stick around a while longer.' He resumed sipping as though he hadn't completely ripped her good intentions to pieces.

Violet could barely find the words to refute his allegations. She'd never expected to have to justify caring for him. 'I... I... That's not fair. I only came back for you. To make sure you were all right.'

'Unfortunately for you, and me, I'm fine.'

She was sure her frown matched her father's as she struggled to work out what the hell he meant. Were things so bad that he didn't want to be here any more? Was that the reason he'd refused treatment and insisted on leaving hospital too early? A chill blasted through her at the thought of losing another parent to the jaws of that black dog that had hounded her mother to her death.

'You're not fine. You're recovering from a heart attack and you're drowning in a sea of debt. All I want to do is help you.' Her voice hitched as she held out that olive branch. Despite everything, he had to be her main priority now or she would end up truly alone for ever.

He very carefully set his spoon down and fixed her with that withering stare that made Violet want to hide under the table. 'What do you know about my personal affairs?'

Only now, faced with the prospect of telling him what she'd been up to over the past few days, did she realise how intrusive he'd find her actions. She gulped. 'We found the bills and final demands when we were tidying up. It wasn't as if we were snooping.'

'What do you mean "we"? Who else has been prying into my private business?' He was red in the face, building up to one of his eruptions, and Violet braced herself to take the full force of it.

'Nate. He has some really good ideas about what we could do here—'

The fist came down hard on the table, rattling the dishes and the cutlery in its wake. Even Violet was shaking from the impact.

'Who the hell do you think you are coming back here and rifling through my things? Nothing at Strachmore is any of your business. You made that clear when you ran away, Violet. And it certainly has nothing to do with *him*.'

'I understand why you're angry at me. I stayed away too long, I realise that, but why do you hate Nate so much? He saved your life.'

'I didn't ask him to.'

There it was again, the unmistakable sound of a man who'd grown tired of living. She'd dealt with enough suicidal teens in her time to take his comments seriously and not simply dismiss them as attention-seeking. Lord Dempsey would never willingly admit defeat unless there was something seriously wrong.

'Dad—'

The doorbell chimed before she could query his

state of mind any further or tell him how selfish that kind of thinking was.

'You'd better get that. Or do you expect me to struggle all the way to the front door and back?' Apparently the invalid card was only valid if it involved her guilt.

Violet made her way to the door on somewhat shaky limbs. Trying to get her father to open up would be like death by a thousand paper cuts—slow, with each new wound more painful than the last. Whoever was on the other side of this door, be it the Taylors or a door-to-door salesman, she intended to drag them inside to interrupt the direction the conversation with her father was taking. Neither of them were ready to tackle that head-on without building up their strength first.

'Hi. I thought I should pop over and see how the ground lay. Should I get my flak jacket from the car now or have you laced his tea with sedatives already?' Nate greeted Violet with a joke in an attempt to hide the nerves that had kept him from knocking on the door for the past ten minutes.

He'd stayed in the car with the engine running, contemplating whether or not to get involved in the Dempseys' domestics. He'd had no doubt the two of them under the same roof was causing friction when it was in their nature to rub each other up the wrong way. The reservations had come when he'd pictured himself in the middle of it. In the end, his conscience had rapped on the door for him. He couldn't leave Violet to manage his patient and his moods alone. Not when he kept promising her otherwise.

'Oh, Nate. You're a sight for sore eyes.'

He had no room for preening when he saw Violet

was visibly shaken and as pale as the alabaster statues in the entrance hall behind her.

'What's happened?' The whole idea had been to make this a casual visit but he was well versed in emergencies too.

'He's angry about me being here…about our meddling in his affairs…and he's saying such morbid things. It's as if he's upset he's still here.' Violet was hanging on to his arm as she rambled. There was absolutely no danger of him leaving now.

'Okay. We knew he wasn't going to react well when he found out we'd been digging into his financial status. As for the rest, depression or anxiety isn't uncommon in heart-attack survivors. He'll be feeling weak and vulnerable. Something which your father definitely won't be used to. He might need to start a course of anti-depressants. I'll have a chat with him and see if I can get a handle on his mental state.' Another reason Nate would've preferred he'd prolonged his hospital stay. There were so many possible after-effects, and not all of them physical, aftercare was a vital part of recovery. He'd been denied giving that and Violet was the one suffering as a consequence.

'That would usually be where I come in.' Violet sighed as she stepped aside to let him in, looking as dejected as she was describing her father.

'Hey, it's not your fault. You're too close to see this objectively and you're doing your bit simply by being here.' He hooked a finger under her chin to lift her head up and was tempted to kiss her worried mouth to bring them both some comfort.

It seemed an age since they'd last done that, their night together almost nothing more than an erotic fantasy now. He'd wanted that intimacy again, even for the briefest moment, to remind him it had been real, that she'd wanted him once as more than someone to bail her out when the going got tough.

'Who is it?' The dulcet tones of a crotchety Earl soon put paid to any romantic notions, reminding Nate of his professional responsibilities.

The medical stuff was within the remit of his normal day-to-day life. Whatever this was with Violet certainly wasn't. He let his hand fall down to his side again and took a deep breath. 'I guess it's time to face the music.'

Violet led the way towards the dining room with no real urgency in her step and he could see her steeling herself before she went in. It had never been the homely environment he'd been lucky to have even before his strained relationship with his parents, but the atmosphere here was so tense and thick with resentment it wasn't conducive to anyone's health.

'Hello, Lord Dempsey. I was just down visiting my parents and I thought I'd see how you were settling in.' It was a little white lie to soften the idea of his trespassing where he wasn't wanted. In all these years he'd never just 'popped in' for a visit, even when he'd been only a stone's throw away.

Samuel Dempsey eyed the offer of a handshake with a suspicious glare. 'I don't need to settle in. *I* live here.'

'I know Violet has been very worried about you—'

All concerns were brushed aside with an ungentlemanly snort.

'Worried about her inheritance more like. Is that why you're *really* here? Violet tells me you've both been helping yourselves to things while I've been fighting for my life.' He leaned back in his chair, arms folded across his chest, giving the impression he was enjoying this power play. It was as though he saw this as a game, where they were competing for the title of top dog and there could only be one winner. Nothing could be further from the truth. Nate wanted them to work together to make sure he was still fit to rule his kingdom.

'That's not what I said. We were simply trying to get things organised for you coming home.' Violet made a futile attempt to clear their names. Futile because her father wouldn't even look at her while she was talking, keeping his beady eyes firmly tableside on Nate.

'I've got your number. You're teaming up to snatch this place from under me. I see you riding around in your fancy car pretending you are somebody. Well, let me tell you, class isn't something you can buy.' The blue veins were pulsing beneath his flushed skin as he raged against his imagined foes.

Nate had to count to ten in his head to keep his own temper in check. It wasn't his place to make this any more personal than it already was by pointing out the Earl's faults in turn. Class didn't always equate to decency and it was entirely possible to have one without the other.

'Please don't do this again, Dad.' Violet's small plea was so full of fear it instantly made Nate think of her caught in the middle of her parents' battles. He didn't want to put her in that position again and he certainly didn't want to inflame the situation any further.

'It's okay, Violet. Your father's entitled to say how he feels in his own home.' It was a shame he'd never let his daughter do the same. Still, it wasn't his family, or his battle.

'Damn right I am. Just as I'm entitled to some privacy. I shouldn't have to put my personal correspondence under lock and key every time I leave the house.' For a man so predisposed to dramatic outbursts, he was doing a good job of making his near-death experience sound like a trip to the shops. Painting Nate and Violet as a pair of opportunistic burglars in the process.

'Perhaps I should leave.' Nate made eye contact with Violet. Her father wasn't showing any signs of having given up on life, at least not to him. If anything he seemed to be fighting to hang on to everything he had.

'Good idea. I've been perfectly capable of taking care of myself for the past I-don't-know-how-long. I don't need anybody's help now.' The Earl was clinging desperately to his independence.

Nate could sympathise to some extent with his stubborn stance against them. They were essentially trespassers who'd taken it upon themselves to get involved in his affairs. But he could also see that Violet was simply doing what she thought was best for him. This had moved so far beyond the professional excuses he'd made for coming here tonight he was in danger of having his say on the matter. Something that probably wouldn't please either side and would only drag him in deeper.

'Everyone in this room knows that's not true. You have no money coming in and nothing to cover the debts you already have. I've managed to cover a few of the most urgent bills but you need to generate some sort of income.' Whether it was because she'd found strength in numbers or she was so exasperated, Violet was starting to find her voice. She didn't need him; she hadn't done for some time. Nate imagined it was a case of reverting back to type because she had so much unfinished business with her father. And him.

'I didn't ask you to pay for anything. I suppose the money came from Dr Flash here? Well, the Dempseys don't need anyone's charity. Especially not from domestic staff.'

'I paid with my own money. I sold Mum's necklace, if you must know. One of us had to get our priorities straight.'

Nate could only stand and watch as Violet threw herself under the bus to save him from further abuse. Now she had her father's full attention.

'How could you?' He visibly paled and sat up straighter in his chair with her full disclosure, acting as though it were a betrayal rather than the huge sacrifice Nate knew it had been for her.

'What's the alternative? Wait for the bailiffs to seize it anyway in lieu of payment? Or do you have a Swiss bank account somewhere you've forgotten to mention?'

Violet was in full flow now. There was no reason for Nate to intervene when she was managing so beautifully without back up. She needed to have her say. It had been a long time coming.

'Does her memory mean so little to you that you can sell it for a few pieces of silver?'

'If you knew Mum at all you'd realise she hated those gaudy baubles you insisted on buying her. It was sentimental things like the clay bead bracelet I made at primary school she wore every day, not expensive statement jewellery.'

Not unlike the bracelet she'd worn on her own wrist for over a decade. There was a flutter of something he didn't want to recognise in his chest at the thought he'd held the same special place in her thoughts. It felt a lot like hope.

'Your mother was a good woman. She deserved the best.'

'But at what price, Dad? She knew you couldn't afford that kind of expense and worried herself to death over it. I think she'd be only too happy at the idea of using it to make a difference here.'

It was the first time Nate had witnessed something approaching shame on the Earl's face before he hung his head. 'I know you blame me, Violet, but your mother was a sick woman. I can't change what happened in the past.'

Violet dropped to her knees and reached for her father's hand. 'But you can do something about the future. We can open Strachmore to the public and bring enough money in to cover all your outgoings here. Nate's been looking into the idea of hiring part of the place out as a wedding venue.'

Just when it seemed as though they were making progress, Samuel Dempsey got to his feet, almost knocking his daughter to the floor in the process.

'Over my dead body! This is my home. It's not for sale or rent and neither is my pride.'

Nate immediately went to Violet's aid and helped her up to a more dignified position. It was too much of an insult against her good intentions to simply let him get away with this one. He turned, fully prepared to wade in and add his voice to Violet's cause, only to find the Earl had his eyes closed, refusing to entertain further discussion. He truly was the most infuriating man to try and get through to.

Then Nate noticed his hand move to his chest, then

grab his left arm before he fell to the floor with a sickening thud.

'Dad!'

His expletive was drowned out by Violet's shout.

Along with the Earl's sickly pallor and clammy skin, all the signs pointed to another cardiac arrest. Nate should've seen this coming but he'd been too caught up in other people's emotions to keep his doctor head in the game.

Although the Earl had dropped like a stone he'd thankfully avoided hitting the table on the way down and there was no indication of any head injuries. Nate loosened the shirt around his neck and tilted his head back to check his breathing. Nothing.

'He's not breathing. Phone 999.' He delegated phone duties to prompt Violet into moving. He couldn't afford to have her in shock too. Far from helping, his meddling had simply caused more catastrophe. He should've left well alone and they might all have carried on down their own paths they'd chosen a dozen years back. Oblivious to each other's emotional dysfunction.

If he hadn't still been hung up on Violet and insisted on getting involved in her father's treatment in the first place this could've turned out differently. The Earl might've accepted help easier or sooner without all of this added stress.

Leaving the past unresolved now seemed a better option than being directly responsible for his death. If the worst happened there was no chance Violet would ever forgive him, never mind love him.

CHAPTER SIX

VIOLET STAMMERED OUT the address and the details of what had happened to the switchboard operator. It was difficult to focus on what was being said on the other end of the phone when she was watching Nate pump life back into her father's chest for a second time. The difference now was there was no defibrillator to shock the heart back into rhythm. He was literally the only thing standing between her father and certain death.

'The ambulance is on its way.' Sooner rather than later, she hoped. Every second counted now in bringing her father back.

Violet was helpless in the fight, watching her father's body jerk with every violent chest compression needed to keep the blood circulating around his body. It was her fault they were all in this situation. If she hadn't come back in the first place, or dragged Nate into their family politics, her father might still be recovering in his hospital bed. Not lying here on his dining-room floor literally heartbroken because of the accusations she'd thrown at him. This was what happened when she finally stood up to him.

He'd never forgive her for this. If he made it through. She'd never forgive herself if he didn't.

'Did they say how long on that ambulance?' Nate was breathing heavily, sweat beading on his upper lip, with the continued effort of CPR. It was easy to forget how physical a task it was doing the heart's job when it was out of commission.

'Five minutes. Apparently there's one not too far from here.'

Nate nodded and turned his attention back to his patient.

Watching him work, his hair falling over his forehead as he tried to prolong life, was impressive and mesmerising. She, on the other hand, was standing here like a spare part with no active role in saving her father's life.

'Do you want me to take over for a while?' Her mouth was dry at the mere thought of undertaking such a crucial task but Nate needed a break and she needed to do something useful.

'Are you sure?' His serious face told her he wasn't going to leave his post unless she was confident she could do this.

'Yes.' She knelt down beside him on the floor, not giving her brain time to start overanalysing everything that could go wrong.

'Remember, you need to be forceful to be effective. Ready?' He scooted over so she could move closer for the transfer.

'Yes.' No.

She'd never performed CPR on an *actual* person, only synthetic dummies whose fate didn't affect anyone. If she screwed this up she'd have her father's death on her conscience for ever as well as Strachmore's fate.

She locked out her arms and linked her fingers in

preparation, throwing her weight into the first compression when she took over.

'One, two, three…' She counted out each chest pump to keep the timing regular and her brain occupied.

'That's good. Nice and steady.' Nate laid a hand on her back to support her and used the other to grab his phone from his pocket.

Her father's skin was cold beneath her fingers and she tried desperately not to convince herself it was already too late but Nate wouldn't give up and neither would she.

'Come on. We can do this,' she told him in the hope he would suddenly bat her away and tell her he could do this on his own. This was the first time she'd actually been in a position to help him and she prayed it wouldn't be the last.

'Apparently the ambulance is coming up the drive. I'll go out and direct them here if that's okay with you?'

'Sure. Hurry.'

Her arms were beginning to tire with the tension and repetitive movements but adrenaline was keeping them moving. She could hear the sirens, see the shadows of the ambulance lights dancing through the windows, but she didn't relax until Nate returned with the crew, giving them the lowdown on events to date.

'We can take over from here.' Nate gave her a reprieve and took over the compressions while the paramedics set to work with the oxygen and defibrillator.

'Stand clear.'

This time Violet was there to witness the shocks as they were delivered in between Nate's chest compressions as everyone crowded around to save her father's life. They had him hooked up to so many machines and life-saving equipment he might as well have been in the hospital.

After the second shock was administered there was a renewed flurry of activity.

'We've got a pulse.'

'Lord Dempsey, can you hear us?'

'Open your eyes for us, Samuel.'

'Dad?' Violet held her breath, waiting for confirmation there was still a chance he could make it. Nate came to her and put her mind at ease with a squeeze of her hand.

'He's breathing on his own again. You did an excellent job, Nurse Dempsey.'

'We made a good team, Dr Taylor.' Her limbs were shaking as the tension began to ebb from her body, only to be replaced with shock at what she'd just undertaken. They were a long way from celebrating just yet but they'd done their bit to get him this far.

'I'll ride with you in the ambulance in case there are any complications. We might have to operate this time to prevent this from happening again.' Not even Nate's warmth could prevent the cold chill that ran down her spine. They were right back at square one, with the stakes higher than ever. This time she was directly responsible for putting her father in hospital and it was down to Nate again to save the day.

Nate had been more forceful about the need to perform emergency angioplasty as soon as they reached the hospital to prevent any more attacks. This latest episode had obviously shaken the Earl as he'd agreed without much of a fight this time. Now Nate's blue scrubs were sticking to the sweat on his back. He performed this procedure as a matter of routine but not usually on people who thought he'd somehow forged his qualifications, and not with old girlfriends sitting outside waiting for news.

With the Earl awake and aware of everything going on around him, Nate was under pressure more than ever to prove himself. He'd never been more aware of the small risks involved in this minimally invasive treatment, or his responsibilities during it, as he stood over Violet's father.

'Okay, Lord Dempsey, you'll be awake during the procedure but you shouldn't feel anything with the local anaesthetic we've given you. You can even watch what's happening on the monitor beside you.' He usually tried to make his patients more at ease by remaining on first-name terms but he didn't want to antagonise his patient before they started.

'Thanks.'

They'd administered a mild sedative along with a local anaesthetic but Nate was still pleasantly surprised at how co-operative the patient was being, considering his earlier mood. Well, at least less combative than he'd expected. He'd had visions of having to strap him down to stop him taking a swing at him for bringing him back to the hospital.

'We're just going to insert a catheter into the small incision we've made in your wrist. That will allow us to inject X-ray dye into the arteries so we can get a clear picture of what's going on in there.' He could make a better assessment of how to proceed when he could see the problem for himself instead of guessing.

Once he had the nod, Nate carried on as he would

normally do. There was nothing out of the ordinary about this case if he could set personal history aside and stop thinking about how much was riding on this being a success. Potentially this was his chance of winning the Earl's approval, essential in making his and Violet's lives a little easier. It mattered to him to be accepted when he was spending so much time at Strachmore. With Violet. There was also the matter of professional pride when this was his patient who'd been readmitted only a matter of hours after leaving.

With the help of the monitors, he concentrated on feeding the thin, flexible tube through the blood vessels until it reached the coronary arteries on the heart. It was an intricate process, one which he'd honed over the years. Hence, his continued irritation when people dismissed the skills he'd worked hard to perfect.

'You can see on the screen that your right coronary artery is almost completely blocked, preventing blood flowing to that particular section of the heart.' It was clear now exactly what was causing the problem and, providing there were no objections, he could repair it.

'What's next, Doctor?'

If the Earl's co-operation had taken him by surprise, being referred to respectfully in his professional capacity was nearly enough to knock him off his feet.

'The best thing to open the artery is to insert a tiny balloon and inflate it to let the blood flow. I think in your case we'll also need to use a stent too. It's a small mesh tube that helps support the inner wall of the artery to make sure it remains open once we remove the balloon.'

'Whatever you think's for the best.' He deferred to

Nate with his eyes closed, either too tired to argue or too squeamish to watch.

It enabled Nate to relax a tad without being scrutinised as he threaded the guide wire into the affected artery. The balloon was inflated to widen the artery and squash fatty deposits against the artery wall, the stent expanding with it. Once the stent was open, he was able to deflate the balloon and remove it.

'And that's us finished.' The whole thing had taken just over an hour, a typical time for the procedure but, under the gaze of Lord Dempsey, it had felt like a never-ending test of his abilities.

'Already?' Lord Dempsey was straining to make sure he'd been true to his word.

'Yes. We'll send you back to CCU to monitor you overnight but with any luck you should be back home again tomorrow.' He removed the catheter and the lab nurse applied pressure to the site to prevent any bleeding. Job done with a great degree of satisfaction and relief.

'Thank you, Nathaniel.' The Earl reached out to shake his hand and Nate stood a little taller in his comfy Theatre shoes.

'I think you need to thank your daughter too. She was very much part of the team keeping you alive until you got here.' She deserved some positive recognition from him for once too.

'Violet?'

'She helped me perform CPR until the ambulance reached you. That is one lady determined to keep you around for a while longer.' Nate wanted to put to bed the ridiculous idea that she wanted him out of the way.

No devious gold-digger would have worked so hard to bring him back from the dead.

'I'll talk to her.'

'I think it's about time you did but, please, hear her out this time. She only wants the best for you, and the estate.' He'd held his counsel too long and in his eyes both he and Violet had proved their true intentions over the course of the evening. Despite their resistance to Strachmore and all it stood for, they'd both made a commitment to them in their own way.

He stripped off the lead apron that he'd worn to protect against the X-rays and tossed his surgical gown aside, keen to report back to Violet and share this feeling of after-surgery euphoria with someone for once.

Violet was biting what was left of her fingernails. She inspected her once-beautiful nails, now raggedy, the candyfloss-pink varnish starting to flake. It was funny how quickly frivolous things such as her weekly manicure became insignificant in the grand scheme of things. Nate had reassured her that her father's was a relatively straightforward procedure and she had every faith in him, but her father's health was so precarious she couldn't relax until she saw them both coming out of Theatre.

'Did everything go okay?' Her father was awake, Nate was smiling, but she wanted confirmation all had gone to plan.

'Like clockwork. We're just taking your father back to CCU, if you want to come with us?'

He was so handsome in his scrubs, made even more so with his amazing life-saving skills, Violet was liable to follow him anywhere. Overcome with relief and gratitude, she launched herself at him for a hug. She found solace in the smell of sweat and soap, which told her everything about how hard he'd worked over the course of the last hours. Now the drama was over she wished they were able to take time out in one of their old haunts to decompress and simply enjoy each other's company. Somewhere she wasn't constantly faced with reasons she shouldn't want to be with him.

From the corner of her eye she saw her father struggle to sit up. She instantly let go of her hold around Nate's neck and stepped away from the hunky cardiologist. Even though she was proud of him, it was her natural response to back off, knowing her father would never approve of such a public display no matter what the circumstances and especially with someone he deemed beneath him.

'How are you feeling, Dad?'

'Sore.'

If she'd expected Nate to flick on her father's humility switch while he was in there, she was sadly mistaken. She couldn't bear for him to take umbrage against Nate for any residual pain after all his hard work.

'I'm sure Nate did everything he could—'

'I didn't dispute that. From what I saw in there Nathaniel is a very, very skilled physician but I think I'm entitled to express my discomfort after everything I've been through. Now, if you don't mind, I need some rest.'

Violet could only stand open-mouthed as he was wheeled away.

When she finally regained control of her paralysed body parts she turned to stare at Wonder Doc. 'Did

I imagine that or did my father just pay you a back-handed compliment?'

If so, it was a breakthrough of epic proportions. She'd never heard him praise anyone for anything. It was probably the closest thing to an apology they'd ever hear from him. Violet was pleased on Nate's behalf that he was finally being recognised for his achievements even if she wasn't likely to receive that honour herself.

Nate gave her a wry smile to warm her frozen limbs. 'I told you I was good at what I do.'

'Yes, yes, you are.' That brought all things non-medical to Violet's corrupted mind, forcing her to break eye contact before he saw her lustful thoughts for himself. She knew how good he was at everything he did—she'd had a sample for herself. That taster had only made her crave more.

Nate gave a nervous cough and she got the impression those wayward thoughts hadn't been confined only to her head.

'It's late but you can go to CCU and say goodnight before you leave if you want.' Apparently he'd decided to go with the relatively safe ground of dealing with her father compared to that minefield of their relationship and the boundaries they'd come close to redrawing.

'I'm not sure that's such a good idea. I don't want to push my luck and end up in another row with him after that bombshell. I don't want a repeat of what happened at the house.' Their cosy chats didn't have a great track record. For all the good she'd done so far trying to help, she was tempted to simply let his world collapse around him rather than take any more responsibility for his ill health.

'You saw him for yourself. He's quite mellow at the minute. For him. Although, it might be wise not to mention Strachmore. At all.'

'Message received loud and clear.' Violet pondered his advice. There'd been enough excitement for one day, but surely five minutes spent bedside saying good-night couldn't hurt? It might even put her mind at ease to see him settled at the end of such a traumatic twenty-four hours. Then she might stand a chance of a decent night's sleep.

She set off after the porter towards the coronary care unit safe in the knowledge Nate had fallen into step next to her. She was getting too used to having a sidekick with her during her trials and tribulations. When she finally went back to London she was probably going to have to get a dog or something to pour out her troubles to even though it would be a poor substitute for this man, who knew her better than she knew herself at times.

'I'm just popping in to make sure you're comfort-able before I head home.' Violet approached her fa-ther's bed with as much caution as ever. There never was any warning of what mood he'd be in from one minute to the next, and he was bound to be tired and cranky after the evening he'd had. This wasn't the time or place to start pointing out his flaws and mis-takes again. With any luck he'd begin to realise them for himself some day.

'I know you would rather I'd died instead of your mother. I do too.'

It was such an out-of-the-blue statement coming from him it stunned Violet into silence. Not so long ago it would've been true, she'd have preferred to have lived without him instead of her mother, but she'd moved past that. Nobody could change the past and it had been her mother's decision to leave them when all was said and done.

The greatest surprise, other than her father considering anyone else's feelings, was that he'd expressed something approaching remorse. She guessed facing his own mortality had finally awoken his conscience from its long slumber.

'Why would you say that now when we've done everything we could to keep you here tonight?'

He'd never shown any emotion over her mother's death, not even in the immediate aftermath. He'd done what he'd always done: pretended the bad stuff wasn't happening around him and carried on as usual. That had included hiding the truth from her about the overdose, leaving it to others to break that news to her. Hearing him express a wish to swap places with his dead wife at any point was unexpected, out of character, and made him more human. It went some way to softening the hard stance she'd taken against him because of his apparent indifference to her great loss, but he should be celebrating the fact he was still here tonight.

She eyed Nate, hoping he knew where the hell that had come from. Perhaps he'd done some counselling alongside the heart repairs—a full mind and body MOT.

'Lord Dempsey, are you feeling okay?' Nate's frown didn't tally with insider knowledge of his patient's sudden attack of conscience. Now he'd witnessed that morbid decline for himself he might be able to prescribe something to lift his mood.

'I know you only came home through a sense of duty, Violet. I've barely heard from you in over a decade, for goodness' sake. I could've died tonight without us ever clearing the air and I think it's time we had this talk before it's really too late. You've made it pretty clear you thought I was responsible for you losing your mother but do you honestly think I ever wanted to be here without her? I blame myself for her death as much as you do but I can't change what happened. Lord knows, I wish I could.' He bypassed Nate's question to continue his train of disturbing thoughts, his eyes red with stubborn unshed tears.

Nate pulled the curtains around the bed, giving them some privacy. It merely added to Violet's sense of emotional suffocation.

It was the first time her father had taken any responsibility for her mother's death, everything Violet had wanted since losing her. Seeing his distress as he did so didn't bring her the peace she'd always imagined. Quite the opposite. It was distressing to discover he'd been hurting all this time on his own too. Perhaps if he'd been this open with her back then she wouldn't have been so desperate to leave and they could've used their combined grief as a base to evolve their relationship instead of leaving it to stagnate.

'All you had to do was love us.' Her voice became smaller as the tragedy of her loss got bigger.

'I did. I still do. I never meant to hurt you or your mother but I always wanted to do the best for Strachmore too. Generations of my family kept the castle through war and unrest. I couldn't be the one to let it all slip away. I didn't realise it was your mother I'd truly failed until it was too late.'

'Why couldn't you have said this at the time to your teenage daughter who thought she'd lost the only parent who cared for her?' Until now she'd only ever seen the dark side of him and had run from it at the first opportunity. This guilt, this expression of actual emotion had come too late for her mother, perhaps even for her. Everything she'd thought she'd known about her father and her parents' marriage had coloured her view on every relationship she'd ever had. It had even cost her one with Nate.

'I dealt with things the only way I knew how—with a stiff upper lip. I was devastated, but what use would I have been to you if I'd fallen apart too? I might have gone about things the wrong way but I was the one who had to be strong. I've come close to death too many times this week to take anything for granted. I don't want to die with you still hating me. It's difficult enough knowing your mother went feeling that way about me. I'd do anything to change places with her. I've wanted that since she passed but I can't undo the past. Nathaniel has given me a second chance to at least try and make amends with you.'

Silence fell in the small cubicle, heavy with unspoken apology. She wouldn't have expected him to break down and beg for forgiveness but seeing him contrite like this was unnerving in itself. It was a bittersweet moment. This was the conversation he should've had with her mother, explaining his actions and exhibiting signs of humanity—capable of making mistakes and now owning up to them.

The logical part of her brain knew her mother must've had mental-health problems beyond her father's churlish ways to do what she'd done. Violet had chosen to ignore that fact and diverted all the anger she felt as a result of her mother's actions towards her father. It wasn't going to be easy to shift her perception of her father overnight and she needed time to process everything. With his roundabout apology she wasn't certain what he expected from her in return either.

'I don't hate you and I'll be here for as long as you need me. We'll discuss this again when you're feeling better. Now get some rest.' She was desperately fighting her own tears, her breath catching on the lump of emotion wedged in her throat. She didn't want to cause him any more pain than he was obviously already in.

She leaned over and placed a kiss on his cheek. An act she'd never carried out without being prompted. He wanted her forgiveness, and she would willingly give it if she thought they could move on, but she couldn't help feeling as though she was walking into another trap.

'Are you going to be okay?' Nate had snatched his keys from the dining-room floor where they'd fallen from his pocket during the fight to save the Earl and now he was saying his goodbyes on Strachmore's marble steps.

He and Violet had taken a taxi back together, since he had to get his car, but she'd been non-communicative during the journey home. She was entitled to some quiet after another fraught day. He'd inadvertently intruded on her heart-to-heart with her father and been as shocked by the outcome as she was. However, he didn't want her to sit brooding all night, feeling guilty about what had happened, or dwelling on her father's state of mind. None of this was her fault.

'I never saw that coming,' she said, staring off into

the distance. 'He was grieving in his own way, still is, and I left him alone. I'm supposed to be a mental-health expert and I didn't even consider that a possibility.'

'You couldn't have known when you were in a different country. I would say he's been very good at keeping his feelings to himself when my parents didn't pick up on it either and they see him every day. Hell, he's my patient, if you want to start pointing fingers at people who should have seen he was having trouble coping with his grief.' Perhaps if Nate hadn't known the background to their estrangement he might've picked up on other reasons for the Earl's mood swings besides his relationship with Violet. Blame wasn't going to solve the problem, only more of the plain talking he'd witnessed tonight.

'That's the point, I wasn't here. I was feeling sorry for myself in London, learning to treat people with mental issues when my own father was mourning the loss of his wife. Hating him all this time makes me the awful person I thought he was.' Her eyes rested on him again, two oceans of blue crashing with waves of sorrow.

He grabbed her by the shoulders, desperate to still those troubled waters. 'Stop this. It's obvious he wants you to stay here—that's why he's telling you all of this. He's trying to leave whatever has gone on between you behind so you can now both start to look forward. You've both suffered and I'm sure you've both said things you've regretted but now's the time to let the healing begin. These plans for Strachmore could mean a clean slate and a chance for you two to start building bridges if we can get him on board.'

A strengthening of Violet's relationship with her father would not only bring them some peace of mind, it could also give Nate some space from the happenings at the Dempsey household. He was already in way over his head and if he could hand over the reins so much the better. When all was said and done he wasn't going to be part of Strachmore's legacy any more than he was going to be a permanent fixture in Violet's life. These were all simply temporary arrangements due to circumstance. Not even his first love took priority over his sense of self-preservation. At least, not long-term.

'And I want that but not at the price I suspect I'll have to pay. What if I'm simply swapping one prison for another? I ran away so he wouldn't be able to force me to marry and keep me tied to this place. After that emotional outpouring I'll be the bad guy again if I leave again. I don't want him under the illusion I'm staying indefinitely. Whether he chooses to go along with this wedding idea or not, I've still got a job and a home in London I have every intention of returning to.'

Her torment was pretty much the same as his own. Somehow they had to find a way to fulfil their promises but still maintain their hold on their lives preheart attack. Ones which hadn't included Strachmore or each other.

'Everything's still raw at the minute. You can clarify the situation tomorrow and discuss what you both expect to come from this.' When everyone had had a good night's sleep and some time to think about exactly what they'd committed to.

'I don't know how to do that without disappointing him again. I want Strachmore to succeed but I'm not sacrificing everything else for it.'

'Tell him you're glad he got everything off his chest

but your personal circumstances haven't changed as a result. Set very clear boundaries so you remain in control. If you don't have a firm date for going back to work, make one and don't break it.' That would prevent them both from falling any deeper into this quagmire of guilt and responsibility they'd unwittingly stumbled into. With an end date they'd be able to claw their way back out at some point and carry on as though this had never happened.

'He's always been such a dominant force I don't think I can cope if he starts talking about dying again. I'm afraid I'll let him guilt-trip me into staying permanently. I'm so weak.'

He could feel her shoulders sag under the weight of her burden. Nothing tonight seemed to have eased it for her. He gave her a gentle shake in an attempt to awaken that fighting spirit he'd seen in her earlier.

'Emotionally and physically exhausted perhaps, but you're certainly not weak. You took over CPR tonight without hesitation when I began to tire, pumping your father's heart as though it was your own life depending on it. Does that sound like a woman who can't handle a crisis to you?'

That raised a faint smile. 'I did surprise myself.'

'You didn't surprise me. I've always known how amazing you are.' He let go of his grip on her shoulders to cradle her face in his hands. With only the shine of the moon lighting the darkness, bathing Violet's heart-shaped features in its silvery glow, she'd never looked so beautiful.

With adrenaline and pride still coursing through his veins post-op, he leaned in for a kiss. He'd gained some respect tonight and it was enough to bolster his ego. Although he might never find total acceptance, her soft lips against his would be sufficient reward.

Violet accepted his tongue into her warm mouth, met him with her own. Somehow she tasted sweeter now he knew there'd be no complications in getting involved. She didn't want to stay at Strachmore any longer than was necessary or any more than he did. They could both walk away at the end of her stay without any ill feeling or recriminations this time.

They wanted each other—that much had never really been in doubt. Everything preventing this attraction reaching its natural conclusion was an obstacle constructed by his own pride.

'Are we really going to do this?' Violet already knew the answer but they'd both changed their minds so often she didn't want either of them to end up disappointed. Her head was so full of every word spoken, every life-changing decision that had been made over the course of the evening, she needed to be free of her thoughts for a while.

Nate was encouraging her to leave as soon as feasibly possible, removing that last obstacle before they got naked with each other. They were going into this with their eyes open and their hearts closed this time around. Neither would expect more than the other was prepared to give, avoiding any guilt or misunderstandings. Exactly how she preferred to conduct her love life.

'I guess so.' Nate interrupted her inner conciliation with what she was doing with his husky breath in her ear. It instantly revitalised her weary body, awakening every nerve ending and hitting each erogenous zone simultaneously.

Why was she still waiting?

'Shall we take this inside?' She was breathless; the cold night air and Nate's trail of kisses over the sensitive skin at her neck conspiring to make her shiver.

'Only if we can skip the acrobatics on the fixtures and fittings and go straight to bed. I've been on my feet all night.' Nate grinned as he backed her over the doorstep and kicked the door shut with his foot.

'You're just full of brilliant ideas, Nathaniel Taylor.' She wasn't about to object to some tenderness after the day she'd had. A night lying in each other's arms sounded perfect to her.

'I think this is one of my best ones yet.' He growled and grabbed her backside. She flung her arms around his neck as he kissed her again, keeping them locked together as he hoisted her up around his waist.

'I thought you said no acrobatics?' It did a girl's ego good to be picked up so effortlessly and carried upstairs as though she weighed nothing. Even more when she could feel the hard evidence of her seducer's arousal pressing into her.

'I'm simply making sure I have you where I want you. The door is shut, my phone's off, and I'm not due back to work until tomorrow. No more interruptions. Tonight is ours. I'm reclaiming it.' He fastened his mouth to hers, sealing that promise he would do everything to drive her demons away for a while at least.

'Well, in that case, giddy up, Taylor.' She dropped her hand to slap him on the ass, giggling at the surprise on his face.

'Oh, it's like that, is it, Dempsey? You think you're the one calling the shots here?' He halted their journey at the top of the stairs, pushing her up against the wall and rendering her limbs useless.

'Uh-huh,' she mumbled, daring him to prove her wrong.

Now he had her pinned between the hardness of his body and the brickwork, his hands were free to do just that. He slid the sleeve of her white peasant blouse off her shoulder, exposing her skin to more soft kisses. Her insides turned to mush while everything on the outside stood up and begged for more.

'You sure about that?' he asked with a devilish grin that caught her breath as she waited to see what else he had in store.

'Hmm, mmm.' She nodded, temporarily struck dumb as he slipped his hand inside her bra.

Her nipples were as hard as diamonds now at the very idea he was claiming her body for the night as he palmed her breast with an authority to make her gasp. She could afford to relinquish a little control if it meant feeling this good.

He teased her at first with a flick of the tongue over her puckered pink flesh, only increasing the pressure, and the enjoyment, when she bucked against him demanding more. There were no more thoughts buzzing in her head except those of the carnal kind as Nate drew her nipple into his mouth, sucking her towards oblivion. She was caught between a moan and a gasp as he took her to the crossroads between pain and pleasure.

She'd been right not to let this happen when they were young. If she'd known this would be how it felt to be in his bed she might never have left home. At least here and now she was free to savour this for what it was without trying to predict what happened next. She'd take an orgasm and one hell of a memory to keep her warm in her old age over a doomed relationship any day.

'You're a stubborn so-and-so. I guess we'll just have to take our turn at going on top.' He peeled her back off the wall and carried her towards the bedroom. It was just as well when she knew her trembling legs would never have carried her there on their own.

He dropped her gently onto the bed and proceeded to strip her clothes away, leaving her panties to the very last. If sexy was a handsome cardiologist tugging your underwear down with his teeth she'd hit the jackpot. It was like watching her wildest, most erotic dream play out for real. Except someone had censored out the best bit.

She teased her fingers along the ridge in his trousers, making it his turn to moan. And strip. He stood strong and proud, meeting all of her expectations as he sprang free from his confinement.

'What about contraception? I don't have any with me.' The pained expression as he made the confession said he'd put an end to this now, regardless of his own discomfort, if protection was an issue.

'It's okay, I'm covered.' She might've been offended he was so frightened of somehow getting trapped if she hadn't been on the pill since her first real boyfriend for the very same reason. A pregnancy didn't go together with her independent woman stance.

Nate's relief was there in his smile, and every other part of his body she could see was willing this to happen. There didn't seem a valid argument for holding back any more when they were clearly ready to take the next step. One they'd both waited a long time for.

He joined her on the bed, covering her lips and body with his. She rubbed herself against his erection, her softness yielding to his long length until they were joined together in one quick thrust. He exhaled a shaky breath in her ear as she settled around him. The sound of his contentment echoed the same sense of satisfaction travelling from her well-tended lips to her curled toes. This moment was everything she'd expected it to be, everything she'd feared it could be.

He was kissing her again, tending her lips at a leisurely pace, reminding her they had all night to indulge this fantasy when her body was craving everything he had now. She trembled with need, her urgency to reach that final peak increasing every time he drove into her. Her mind drifted between this plane and the next, only the pinch of Nate's fingers on her flesh keeping her anchored in the present for now.

As their bodies slammed together she made the mistake of looking into his eyes. Regardless of the fact this was supposed to be a one-time-only deal, those eyes were shifting from brown to green, reflecting emotions that weren't included in the terms and conditions. They should've made some sort of 'no kissing on the lips' rule, like Julia Roberts in *Pretty Woman*, to prevent this from being any more than sex. Except they weren't strangers who'd hooked up on the sidewalk and the kissing damage had been done a long time ago.

She tightened her hold on Nate internally and externally, hitching her legs around his waist and clenching around him. They needed to start treating this like hot, dirty sex, not childhood sweethearts who'd finally consummated their feelings for one another.

She clung to him, dug her nails into his back, picking up the pace and trying to stop this from turning into something it wasn't. His irises were now only full of desire, dark with lust and need, his breathing erratic as she pushed him towards surrender. This was all about one thing now—sexual release—and that was exactly how she preferred it.

Nate's entire body shuddered against her as he cried out. Finally Violet was able to give herself completely over to the moment as their bodies rocked together one last time. All of the tension and stress she'd been carrying inside flowed away as she threw herself into that welcoming abyss.

She didn't even know she was crying until Nate wiped her tears away.

'Hey. Was it really that bad?' Not once had he seen her break down during everything she'd faced since coming back here. Although she'd come close to cracking at times, she'd held it together with every new challenge her father's illness had brought her. To see her break now pained him when they'd shared something amazing together. Society ranking had meant nothing when they were rocking each other's world and he hoped these weren't tears of regret. Not when he expected her to be soaring up on the clouds with him after what they'd experienced together.

'No. It was really that good. You made me forget all the bad stuff.' She gave him a watery smile.

'My reputation remains intact.' He lay back, hands behind his head, his ego as satisfied as the rest of him.

'Definitely. I guess it all caught up with me for a

moment.' She turned her face away from him as though she was embarrassed she'd let him see her cry.

Nate turned on his side and pulled her close. There was no reason for her to feel ashamed when lesser mortals would have struggled long before now. Still, he didn't want to draw any more attention to her tears when she was uncomfortable about it.

'In that case it's my duty to keep you occupied— body and soul. I do believe it's your turn to go on top.' He rolled over, taking Violet with him so she could feel as though she was back in control for a while.

He'd spent a long time imagining this time with her and he didn't want anything to spoil it for either of them. They'd already shared the lows of today, they were entitled to enjoy a few highs too. Tomorrow they'd have to face all of those same problems keeping them tied to the estate, but tonight was still theirs.

CHAPTER SEVEN

THE RIGOROUS BEDROOM workout might have taken Violet's mind off everything except what Nate was doing to her body, but it hadn't helped her sleep any easier. She sat up watching his broad chest rise and fall in peaceful slumber as the sun rose.

He had a body made to help a girl forget—those perfect pecs, lickable abs, and…damn she needed him gone. Lying here naked together wasn't going to help matters one iota. Bedding him once had been exciting, eye-opening, leaving her curiosity and body satiated, but ringing the bell for round two was only asking for trouble. It had been easier to tell herself this would be a one-off before she'd known how good they were together.

This wasn't her usual casual affair where no feelings above the waist came into play. Never mind he was involved in everything going on between her and her father, now he'd seen her cry, for goodness' sake. She never cried, not in front of anyone, and certainly not during sex. It was a wonder he hadn't bolted out of the door at the sight of the first tear. In fact, it was kind of disturbing he hadn't. If this was purely sex, why was he still here?

Nate rolled over, the sheet falling lower to display that sexy 'V' of his torso leading to the danger zone. She dragged her eyes away with more discipline than she'd known she possessed. Good sex was like any other addiction—hard to resist when it could make your troubles fade away so easily and leave you feeling invincible. It was the side effects you had to watch out for. Emotional attachment had a way of sneaking into temporary 'fixes'.

She sneaked another peek at Sleeping Beauty, who was definitely beginning to stir beneath the covers. There was absolutely no chance of going cold turkey when she was going to be exposed to said addictive substance every day here. Only the sound of the front door opening stopped her from falling off the wagon before she'd even got on it and taking one last hit of that Nate Taylor good stuff.

'Cooee!' It was closely followed by the morning call of the lesser-spotted housekeeper.

Violet had forgotten the Taylors had more than one set of keys between them. They always rose with the larks to start their duties and let themselves in so as not to disturb the Earl before he was ready to wake. Apparently those same rules didn't apply to her. She wasn't used to having to answer to anyone except herself these days.

'It's only me!' Mrs Taylor called again, louder this time, as though she was getting closer.

There'd be no way of passing this off as anything casual if Nate's mother caught them in bed. They'd never hear the end of it. Although her father had begun to warm towards Nate, if he found out about this all hell would break loose.

'Wake up!' she whispered and shook her bed partner awake.

'Hmm?' His eyes fluttered open with a moan that almost made her care less about getting busted. Almost.

She scrabbled around the floor for her discarded clothes and hastily threw them on. She might think more clearly if she wasn't naked. Or lying next to Nate's impressive morning glory.

'Your mother's here.'

That woke him up and killed his libido quicker than a bucket of ice-cold water.

'What?' He bounced up, wide-eyed now and with that same look of panic he'd had when she'd once caught him skinny dipping in the lake. Unfortunately Violet hadn't had as clear a view of his assets then as she did now as he hopped around the room trying to get dressed.

'Violet? I wanted to make sure everything was all right. Have you seen Nathaniel this morning? I see his car's still parked outside—' Mrs Taylor voiced her concerns from somewhere on the stairs.

Nate muttered all the expletives running through Violet's head at the same time. The first rule of secret liaisons was to be discreet. History should have told them privacy wasn't an option around here.

'How the hell are we going to get out of this one?' He jammed his feet into his shoes, the muscles in his back flexing with tension. He'd always been a completely different person when he was around his parents than when he was with her. In this case his frustration was most likely directed at himself and her for letting this happen.

'I've got an idea. Stay here.'

He was so straight-shooting he might well stomp out and announce what they'd done to shock his mother and get her to back off. Violet didn't want them making this into a big deal simply because they'd been interrupted.

She stepped out of the room before he could grab her and tiptoed to the top of the stairs. 'Hello, Mrs Taylor. Nate stayed over in the west wing last night. It was late when we got back from the hospital and he'd left his car here. I thought it would be better for him to stay than drive home when he was so exhausted. I'll give him a call and perhaps you could make us something to eat in the meantime?' She hated using her position here to suit her agenda, the lies made her sick to the stomach, but in this instance she deemed them necessary, for everybody's sake.

'Of course, dear.' Mrs Taylor beamed, no doubt thrilled at the idea of resuming her duties to the family in the Earl's absence. Violet couldn't imagine one without the other any more, nor did she want to. The Taylors were part of Strachmore and would hopefully take the reins when she was no longer here.

Violet waited until Mrs Taylor scurried off towards the kitchen before she turned back. Nate was fully dressed now and standing by the door with a scowl to sour the milk his mother was probably pouring on their cornflakes. She suddenly found the need to justify her actions. After all, this was his family she was bossing about.

'I thought it would buy us some time.'

'Sure. There's nothing Mum loves more than playing the faithful servant. I guess I'll see you downstairs for breakfast in five.'

It was her turn to be dismissed and she didn't enjoy it one bit. The fairy tale was well and truly over and now they were back to that upstairs-downstairs divide that had always dominated their lives.

Nate doubted there was anything more cringeworthy than a post-coital breakfast with an ex and your mother. When had his life got so messy? Oh, yes, the second Violet Dempsey had walked back into it wearing skin-tight jeans and a worried smile.

'I'm so glad things went to plan with your father at the hospital. I hardly slept a wink last night.'

Nate declined a second cup of tea. He'd only agreed to this charade so his mother's suspicion was kept to a minimum and he wouldn't be expected to pay penance for defiling the Earl's daughter.

'Neither did I, Mrs Taylor.' Violet's reply was innocent enough for his mother's ears. To his, it was a reference to something definitely inappropriate for the breakfast table. Something that was now reminding him of everything they'd done last night instead of sleeping, in all its X-rated glory.

'Speaking of which, I'm going to have to nip home and change before I go into work and check on him.' He drained the last of his tea and took a big enough bite of toast to reassure his mother he'd eaten. Her fussing wasn't confined solely to the Dempseys' welfare but he didn't have to pay for the privilege.

It hadn't sat well with him when Violet had requested she make breakfast for them. Deep down he knew it had been a ploy to save their blushes, but it had succeeded in also reminding him of his place too in the scheme of things. Although he still couldn't quite believe they'd finally slept together, he wouldn't let his ego get too inflated. He was always going to be the son of the hired help, no matter how big his pay packet.

'Thanks for everything you did last night.' This time he knew she was deliberately trying to make mischief as she fixed him with those ever-darkening sapphire eyes.

She pursed her lips together to blow the steam from her china cup and Nate's mind immediately connected her actions to scenes of a sexual nature. He jumped up from the table, lucky it was only his knee banging against the table in the process.

'You're welcome. Any time.' They hadn't discussed what happened next with regard to this new development in their relationship, but something told him it was going to take a great deal of willpower to prevent it happening again. That something was going to require a long cold shower to get rid of.

At least she hadn't seen him off to work with a packed lunch and a kiss in that we've-slept-together-so-let's-set-the-wedding-date fashion some were fond of after one night in bed. He'd met enough of those to recognise the hope of commitment even with a promise of none. He should be happy Violet didn't have it, not lingering on his Dempsey-induced inferiority complex. It left the bedroom door open for another casual hook-up with no expectations beyond those four walls. If she was agreeable, continuing the more physical side of their relationship for the time she had left at Strachmore could be the ideal way to work out their residual issues and finally get closure.

Today's status update: *Lover*.

* * *

It had all but killed Violet sitting so close to Nate this morning, pretending they hadn't spent the entire night getting to know each other more intimately than ever before. While they'd swapped their private thoughts and feelings in their younger days, it was nothing compared to what they'd shared together in bed. Sex with Nate had been the only positive experience she'd had since coming home, and the most fun.

She didn't know what new discoveries she'd make regarding her father from one day to the next but so far they'd all taken an emotional toll. Her time with Nate had been cathartic, a chance to wind down and remember how it was to be a young, carefree woman. She could do with more of that. More of him.

His mother's interruption this morning had prevented them from analysing their actions and discussing where they went from here. With her body still zinging from their tryst, she hoped he was on the same page she was as far as letting this thing run its course. The only commitment she'd intended making was to her job back in London with a phone call today.

Although her father's altered attitude was a revelation, she'd discovered for herself it hadn't made him Dad of the Year overnight. His old, grouchy self was very much alive and kicking when she'd been to see him this morning. She'd left him talking to the rehabilitation team and come back to make a start on making Strachmore accessible to the public in the hope he'd agree to give the idea a chance. The first step was a deep clean of the areas she thought might appeal to history buffs. Mrs Taylor ensured the main house was spick and span but it had been some time since any-one had paid any attention to the old servant quarters.

This part of the house where her ancestors had housed their domestic staff had always intrigued her and she'd used it as a hiding place at times, safe in the knowledge her parents would never venture there. The major flaw in the architecture here was the lack of ven-tilation. She stripped off the denim shirt she'd found in her closet so she was cooler in her strappy white sin-glet as she worked, moving from room to room with her duster and mop.

It was like being in a time warp once you set foot on those stone steps. The period pieces of furniture and personal effects left from days gone by were still in good condition under their thick layer of dust. From the huge wooden table in the servant hall where the staff would've congregated for their meals, to the sparsely furnished bedrooms, they'd all played an important part in Strachmore's history.

She was cleaning down the worktops in the room where the butler used to polish the household's shoes and boots when she thought she heard footsteps. The idea of seeing past residents had never frightened her, but she held her breath as the steps grew closer and louder.

'Thank goodness, it's you.' She let out a relieved sigh when Nate stepped into view, but her heart didn't beat any slower. He was the quintessential gentleman today, again dressed in his dapper charcoal-grey fitted waistcoat and trousers. Although, she preferred him wearing only a sheet. Or not.

'Everyone seems so happy to see me today. It makes a

change. Even your father managed to be civil.' He joined her in the small space, stealing more of her oxygen.

She bustled away to the farthest side of the room to clean the sink so she could breathe again. 'You saw my father?'

'I did. I can't lie and say trying to discuss treatment was a fertile exercise, but he has agreed to see a grief counsellor.' He skirted around the leather-covered bench in the centre of the room to come towards her.

She scrubbed the sink a little harder and tried to avoid his gaze. Her morning had been productive but less than glamorous. If she was to convince him another tumble in the sheets was a good idea she wasn't going to do it covered in dirt and sweat.

'That's great. I really appreciate you doing that for him. It will help him move on.' And her, if they could start some dialogue over what had happened to her mother without blaming each other.

'I really do think he's beginning to soften, though, and it shouldn't be too long before you can persuade him about the benefits of Project Wedding Venue.' He slipped his hands around her waist and made her drop her scrubbing brush.

Was he simply more tactile because he was celebrating their future liberation from Strachmore, or making a move? She wasn't sure if her now supercharged libido was interpreting his actions to suit her needs.

'I…uh…can't wait. That's partly why I'm down here. I thought if we got this cleaned up we could do house tours to break us in gently.'

'You are rocking this domestic goddess thing you've got going on.'

Her mouth was dry now and it wasn't down to the dusty atmosphere. He was nuzzling her neck, holding her tight and giving her the unmistakable sign now that he was interested in picking up from where they'd left off last night. Every step she took with Nate, as much as she wanted it, was also a test of her courage. It was a step further from her comfort zone, and one closer to keeping her here.

'There's so much to do to get the place ready. The paint's peeling everywhere, it'll all need to be redone. Then there's the structural repairs if we don't want to be sued by people getting hit by pieces of loose masonry.' All things that could be remedied easily but suddenly seemed so important to excuse her current state.

'Don't worry—I'll help. We'll all chip in when and where we can while we're waiting for approval from up above.' He spun her around to face him and she forgot why she cared so much about her appearance when he so clearly appreciated it.

He was kissing her neck, grazing her earlobe with his teeth and generally turning her into a puddle of hormones.

'I didn't think I'd see you today. I thought you'd be busy with work.' She was sure he'd be able to feel her pulse throbbing violently beneath his lips.

'I've no patients scheduled for the next few hours. I thought we could take the time to discuss our new *arrangement*.' He dropped a feather-light kiss on her lips.

'What's that?' Violet was burning so hot for him all these wooden fixtures and fittings were becoming a serious fire hazard, but she wasn't going to be the one to make the rules. After the way things had ended the last time between them she wanted this to be his call.

'We had such a good time last night, I don't see any reason to keep us from doing it again. I'd go as far to say we should do it every night before you leave.'

Before you leave. They were the crucial words she wanted to hear. That way there was no room for misunderstandings when her time here was done.

'Every night, huh?'

'Maybe every day too if we feel the need.' He would definitely have the need for her in his arms, night and day, now he'd established a clear time frame. His commitment would end the minute she was on a flight back to London and that was an even bigger aphrodisiac than seeing Violet get her hands dirty.

He'd spent the morning flitting between arousal and annoyance every time he'd thought about last night and this morning. So much so he'd been in danger of becoming distracted. For the sake of his patients, and his sanity, he'd needed to come and see her here. He hadn't known what action he should take regarding their tryst, whether it was better to draw a line under it or repeat it. One look at Violet had made it a no-brainer. Literally. That wasn't the part of his body doing his thinking any more.

'It might make my time here more bearable, I suppose...' She was teasing him now. He could see through that flimsy shirt she was as turned on as he was.

'I think I'll make that my new tagline on my business cards. Dr Nathaniel Taylor—making life more bearable for over thirty years.' He hadn't come here with sex on his mind, only a desire to see her, but the time limit they'd just set meant he didn't want to waste any more time talking.

He planted his lips on Violet's with an urgency he'd never felt with anyone but her. It was an all-consuming need to be part of her, have her be part of him, which he could indulge now he knew there'd be no consequences or regret.

They were a flurry of hands and clothes as they tore at each other's clothes. The waistcoat had been a spur-of-the-moment decision this morning, one he was now cursing for its many, many buttons.

'Sod it.' He tore it open, the damnable buttons pinging around the room in the process.

'Shouldn't it be my clothes you're tearing off?' Violet helped him undo those of his shirt in double-quick time so he was topless, and halfway to where he wanted to be.

'Don't worry, you're next.' He whipped off her shirt in one swift move to find she'd gone commando, her perky breasts greeting him without restraint.

Violet writhed beneath him as he buried his head in her cleavage, revelling in her softness. She was opening his belt, unzipping his fly and letting his trousers pool around his feet. When she gripped his erection in her surprisingly strong hand he had to grab hold of the bench behind him before the instant rush of blood from his head caused him to black out. When she knelt and took him in her mouth there were fireworks in the darkness behind his eyelids.

With her hands gripping his hips, his hands pulling her hair, she took him to the edge of oblivion and back time and time again.

'Come here.' He urged her up beside him to make

this afternoon delight last longer than he was currently anticipating. She kicked off her own jeans and underwear and pressed her naked form against his fevered flesh.

'You know, we're not the first people to make out in here. Rumour has it this was the favourite spot for one of the most notorious butlers who worked here. He had a reputation for seducing the kitchen maids and he carved his initials wherever he made his conquests. They're all over the house. See?' She traced her finger over a set of initials scratched into the leather-covered bench.

He could see where this was going. 'You got a pen-knife on you?'

'There's an old kitchen knife on the window sill.'

He hurriedly carved a crude NT into the wooden cabinets on the wall. 'Now we're making history too.'

'There? Really?'

He pulled her over beside him. 'Well, the randy butler's already claimed the bench and we've done the furniture thing already...'

As much fun as it was marking his territory, he wanted to finish what they'd started. He braced himself against the cupboard doors, caging Violet against the cupboards. His beautiful sex monkey hooked herself around him, permitting their bodies to forge together with ease.

They were so in tune with each other she met his every thrust, kept pace with him until they reached that glorious peak together. Their combined cries of ecstasy were loud enough to wake the dead and Nate was glad they were far enough from the main house to be heard. He didn't often get carried away in such a fashion where anyone, including his mother, could catch him *in flagrante*. His reputation was his livelihood but when he was with Violet nothing else seemed to matter. A dangerous game to play in real life but thankfully this was nothing more than a holiday fling, giving them the excuse to take a walk on the wild side for a week or two.

Once they got their breath back and their clothes back on, Violet returned to the scene of the crime to inspect the graffiti.

'He must've had a lot of fun during his time here. I've seen these initials in the wine cellar, the laundry room and the stone archway at the back of the house.' She studied the carving, lost in thought, as though she somehow envied the freedom of a paid servant.

Nate didn't want her to relate this moment between them to feelings of regret when that was the very thing they were trying to avoid.

'I reckon we could give the horny butler a run for his money. Let's set ourselves a challenge to reclaim every nook and cranny where he's made his mark with one of our own. It shouldn't be Strachmore subordinates only who get to have all the fun. I think it's time the lady of the house got to play too.'

This became more like an illicit romance between servant and mistress with every clandestine meeting in the big house. He could live with that as long as they kept treating this as an exciting fling with a definite deadline. There was no better way to do that than to make love in every room of the house, erasing every bad memory associated with the place in the process. It was therapy on an enjoyable level for both parties, ensuring they chased the pain away with lots of pleasure. A way of closing out the past and opening up their hearts for the future. One that couldn't include each other.

CHAPTER EIGHT

VIOLET DIDN'T KNOW much about *BH* but he'd certainly been a busy boy and *NT* had been doing his best to rival him. Of course, they'd been discreet in recording their exploits for posterity, careful not to vandalise valuable historical artefacts, and they'd had fun along the way. In all, these last two weeks exploring, and supposedly renovating, the forgotten rooms at Strachmore had been some of the best days of her life.

Her father was growing stronger every day, thanks to his work with the physiotherapists and Mrs Taylor's close attention to his diet. Violet had made it clear she'd be returning to her job at the end of the month and that had been sufficient to prompt him into sitting down with her and Nate to discuss the ideas they had to make the estate self-sufficient. He'd eventually agreed in principle to their suggestions and put his signature to the required paperwork for now.

Nate's cool, calm explanation of the proposed changes and the expected benefits had been a crucial part of negotiations. Having him as a third party helped prevent a lot of the emotional obstacles from getting in the way. In the end her father had even offered to sell a few of the paintings he had in storage so she could hire an events manager and whoever else it took to make this thing work in her absence. She might even come home every now and then, now there were a few more attractions, and a few places still left for *NT* to conquer.

There hadn't been a conversation between her and Nate about the possibility of her coming back, or reconnecting if she did. It didn't seem such a stretch to carry on with what they had going on. She wouldn't be a permanent fixture in his life, expecting any more than she did now—great sex. It would be a shame to end things completely when they were having such a good time together. Spending more time with Nate would give her something to look forward to other than TV and pizza at the end of the working week.

She watched him now, schmoozing with the wedding party and the photographer in the grounds, and listened in fascination as he recounted her family's history to the bride and groom. Despite his resistance, he was as much a part of Strachmore as she was. More than ever given their recent antics. She couldn't imagine coming home and not seeing him here.

He waved her over, not ready to leave his post as today's host just yet. The bride and groom were his colleagues from the hospital here to use Strachmore as the backdrop for their wedding photographs. It was a favour both to his friends, and Violet. They got free use of the grounds and it was the first step to gently break her father into the idea of sharing his family home with strangers.

Violet watched the newly-weds smiling for the camera capturing their love for eternity. She wanted to be sick.

'I'd be crying too if I'd been condemned to a life of misery.' She sidled up to Nate, making sure she was out of earshot of the over-emotional couple now dabbing their eyes and hugging. She didn't want to ruin their day but marriage had a lot to do with the misery that had surrounded her ancestral home for so long. Her father's confession of his love for her mother had only served to confuse her views on matrimony further. It had all seemed so black and white when she'd thought her mother's love for her father had never been reciprocated and had cost her her life. The fear of giving everything and receiving nothing in return had kept Violet from falling into that marriage trap.

Now she knew how much her father had loved her and how lost he was without her, it made her question if refusing to admit your feelings was equally destructive. Apparently once love had you in its clutches it was game over, either way, and no amount of pretending or running could prevent it.

'Not a fan of the bride, or the groom?' Nate cocked his head at her as though she were some anomaly of nature for not getting sentimental over the proceedings.

'Marriage in general. You saw what it did to my family. It's all flowers and romance now but she's probably given up all her hopes and dreams to play wifey.' She clung on to that belief her mother had been the only casualty in the marriage—the only one with feelings to consider. The alternative was to admit both of her parents had been at fault and their marriage had been a partnership rather than a dictatorship, with each of them responsible for their own actions. That idea of free will, even as part of a couple, called into question every excuse Violet had ever made for being on her own.

'It's not the eighteen hundreds any more, you know. Women can get married, have children and still work if they choose.' He was being surprisingly pro-commitment for someone who'd taken great care to make sure they didn't have one.

Violet's stomach flip-flopped. Perhaps it was only her he didn't want around long-term. She hadn't contemplated having to see him with someone else any time she came home, someone he might want to settle down with.

'You didn't strike me as the marrying kind.' At least not since they were teenage sweethearts when the intensity of his feelings for her, and hers for him, had sent her running.

'I'm not. It seems to work for some people, though. My parents would be an example of that, I guess. For the record, I have no problem with the honeymoon part. It's being tied down I take issue with.' Nate confirmed his place alongside Violet on the dark side, enabling her to breathe a little easier.

'I don't know who's in your little black book but I'm sure you could find someone who *isn't* into bondage.' Not that she was encouraging him to start hooking up with anyone else. She'd prefer he did that when she was long gone. If he really had to.

Nate snorted. '*That* I can handle. It's this notion that love can solve problems that galls me when, ultimately, it only creates more. All this nonsense is fine for sentimental types whose only aspirations in life are a semi-detached house and two-point-four children but you're right, some of us have bigger dreams.'

She should've been relieved to hear his matrimonial views were in sync with her own but hearing he was as cynical as she was chilled her insides. He was so changed in his views since a teen and she knew she'd been the cause. She must have hurt him more than he ever would admit. Her selfish actions might well have cost him the happy family she'd always thought he'd deserved. The Dempsey curse had struck again.

For a split second she'd zoned out, light-headed and unsteady in her high heels. Her conscience had clearly taken news of his commitment phobia badly, manifesting her guilt physically. They moved with the wedding party through the gardens and she slipped off to take a seat on the carved stone bench under the eucalyptus tree. She stripped a couple of the long blue-green leaves and crushed them in her fingers. The smell of menthol and pine instantly filled the air. She took a deep breath, hoping it would help quell her rolling stomach.

It was coming up to that time of the month too, which probably wasn't helping this feeling of nausea. She did a quick mental calculation—she'd been here for three weeks, her last period had been before she'd taken time off work… She frowned. That couldn't be right. She was as regular as clockwork, every four weeks. Her calculations made it more than five. She did another tot-up of the dates. It was still longer than she'd ever gone. It had to be down to the stress.

Another cramp doubled her over, surely a clear sign all was as it should be. What was the alternative? She hadn't eaten anything other than Mrs Taylor's nutritious meals, same as her father, so it wasn't food poisoning. That left one glaring possibility. She couldn't be pregnant, she just couldn't.

Nate chose that moment to come and sit beside her. 'Are you okay? You look a little pale.'

He put his hand on her forehead, her skin suddenly clammy now. Her own health hadn't been of any significance when her father had been so critical. Now it meant everything. With horror she recalled the fraught night waiting for news of her father and that whole debacle with Nate at the house. Her routine had gone completely out of the window and she'd been a day late taking her pill. In the circumstances she hadn't thought in a million years she would have to take extra precautions. Sex with Nate had never seemed an option. Her recklessness had apparently come at a price after all.

How would she ever make her escape from Strachmore now if she was pregnant? She didn't have the support in London needed to look after a baby and work at the same time and she certainly wouldn't be able to afford childcare on her wages. Nate hadn't asked for this either, when she'd promised him this would be nothing more than a fling. She couldn't expect him to take two of them on when he'd made it clear he didn't even want a plus one. Hell, she didn't even want one.

Parenthood had never been in her future plans. It had been too much for her mother to cope with and not enough for her to stick around. Violet didn't want that level of change, or responsibility, causing chaos in the new life she'd made for herself. Her quiet, organised life, where loving anyone except herself was simply out of the question. It was part of the reason she'd been keen to get back to it, knowing she'd be safe from her feelings for Nate there. Now she was in double trouble.

All she could do was throw herself at her father's mercy now, if the worst had indeed happened, and beg him to take in his pregnant, unmarried daughter. Her life was never going to be the same.

'I think I'm gonna be sick.'

Nate had tried to go after Violet when she'd taken suddenly ill, but she'd shooed him back to the wedding party, insisting someone should be taking an active role in the day's events. He'd had no option but to return to the gathered guests when Strachmore's reputation would soon depend on good word of mouth. Someone had to escort them around the grounds and smile in all the right places. Even if he had been desperate to go check on her.

He'd spent most of his waking moments outside work with her these past weeks, and all of his sleeping ones too. If there was something wrong he wanted to be with her, looking after her the way he always did. He guessed that sense of duty towards the Dempseys was simply born into him. That was the only acceptable explanation for why he cared so much.

Once he'd seen the wedding party off to continue their celebrations elsewhere, he sprinted back to the house. He bounded up the stairs calling her name but she didn't answer. Eventually he found her in her bedroom, changed out of the dress she'd bought specially for today back into her casual jeans and grey hoodie. She seemed even paler now she'd removed her makeup, looking lost perched on the end of her princess bed. He was sorry he'd left her alone for so long.

When he saw her suitcase lying open on the bed, clothes strewn all around, he went into full panic mode.

'What's wrong? Is it that bad? Do you need me to take you to the hospital?'

'I'm fine. Actually, I'm not. I'm far from it but I don't need to go to the hospital. I need to go home.'

She wasn't making any sense and was starting to freak him out.

He knelt on the floor and took her hand. If he'd known she'd react so strongly against the idea of marriage he'd never have suggested bringing his friends here. Her commitment issues were clearly greater than his. In a moment of sentimentality he'd even contemplated how Violet would have looked in a wedding dress. Beautiful and elegant as always, he supposed. If she hadn't run away, breaking his heart, or he'd been enough for her to contemplate staying, they might have had this one day for themselves. It was a shame their parents' actions had skewed their view on marriage for ever when people like his co-workers today seemed to find their happiness in it.

'You don't need to go anywhere. The condemned couple has left the building. We are officially bridal-party free. If it's an allergy to weddings you have, perhaps we can go hang out in the divorce courts to counteract the toxins.' Usually his naff jokes were enough to make her smile, but not today.

'It's not that. Thank you for setting that up today,— they really seemed to enjoy it. It's just…it's just… I can't do this.' She dropped her head into her hands and sobbed her heart out.

This was it—she was going to run again before he was ready to accept it was over. He was supposed to have two more weeks with her. Now she was cutting their time together short he was left with that same sick, empty feeling inside as before. He needed some warning before he was back to his 'work, eat, sleep' routine with none of the fun in between and no one to come home to at the end of the day.

'Do you need me to get you anything?'

'A pregnancy test?' Violet gave a forced laugh, but there was nothing funny about it.

'Don't joke about something like that.'

'I'm not. I'm late.'

Nate dropped her hand to steady himself before he fell over. This couldn't be happening. 'But you're on the pill, right?'

'I think I missed one the night I flew in from London.' Her grimace sucker-punched him in the gut.

'You've been under a lot of stress too though.' He slowly got to his feet, still trying to come up with alternative theories. Ones that wouldn't tie them together for the rest of their days.

'I've been queasy and light-headed today. We both know if there's a possibility the worst could happen, it will. I should have known things were going too well.' The tears started again and it was obvious she didn't want this any more than he did. Neither of them had signed on for parenthood; they hadn't even been able to commit to each other for longer than a month, for heaven's sake.

'We'll get through this. Somehow.' The sickness was spreading to him now, his stomach twisting into a tight knot of anxiety.

A baby, their baby, was going to affect so many—him, Violet, his parents, the Earl... Nobody was going to take the news well. Why should they? He'd messed up big style. He should've taken extra precautions to prevent this happening, but he'd been too lost in his own desires to consider the consequences. Now he'd ruined Violet's future, the one she'd worked so hard to ensure didn't include him.

'I don't expect you to take this on. That's why I'm leaving. This was my mistake. I'll deal with it on my own.' She wouldn't look at him and turned her attention back to throwing her clothes haphazardly into her case.

A vice gripped his heart and squeezed. If there *was* a baby he wanted to be part of its life, wanted to be included in any decisions concerning *their* child. He didn't want Violet to deal with this on her own, regardless of how she did or didn't feel about him. A child needed two supportive parents to have the best possible start in life. To make sure it wouldn't ever feel abandoned, as he had when he'd attempted to improve his lot in life.

'Let's not jump too far ahead of ourselves. First things first—we get a test.' If their lives were about to change for ever they should really find out for sure. The delay would also give him a chance to figure out how to get her to stay. Indefinitely.

The sight of Violet packing to leave had crushed him almost as much as finding her room empty had when she'd first gone to London without an explanation. This was much, much worse. That had been puppy love, a childish infatuation. Now he knew how powerful real love was. The kind that was ripping him apart from the inside out at the thought of her leaving again. She was taking an even bigger part of him with her this time. Literally.

This baby might not have been planned but that didn't mean he didn't want it or wouldn't take responsibility for it. All of those steps he'd taken to avoid emotional attachments had led to the biggest one of all—fatherhood. He got chills every time he thought about it. Twelve years ago this would've been everything he'd wanted. Violet's rejection had changed all that, clouded his view on relationships even more. He'd dodged commitment as if it were some deadly disease when all along he'd still been devoted to Violet. She was the only woman he'd ever imagined spending his life with. Still was.

Unfortunately, the last time he'd confessed his feelings for her she'd skipped the country. He doubted ruining her life with an unplanned pregnancy was going to do anything to improve his chances of her loving him back. She'd only just begun making progress with her father and this news could set them back at loggerheads. Nate knew the Earl's reputation was everything to him and he would never want to sully Violet's name because of his selfish mistake.

The journey in the car to the chemist for the pregnancy test had given him the space and clarity to decide what to do.

'Marry me, Violet.' He loved her. No matter how much he tried to deny it, in the midst of this chaos, the strength of his feelings for her were abundantly clear. Until now he'd refused to admit it and run the risk of repeating the past. Although he'd never be the great love of her life he'd hoped to be, he'd always supported her. He'd always been afraid of marriage but now it seemed the best solution for all three of them. They needed each other.

'Don't be stupid.' A marriage proposal wasn't helping her dizziness as she glared at Nate and back at the screen. She knew it was a knee-jerk reaction to the reading when he'd told her what an awful idea he thought marriage was only hours ago. He didn't love her and she doubted he'd even entertained spending the rest of his days with her until they'd sat on the edge of her bed watching the digital screen spell out their future.

Pregnant
2-3

There was no mistaking her symptoms now, the damage apparently done at the beginning of their supposed fun fling. She gave a strangled laugh. It was either see the irony of that or start crying again.

'I mean it. This baby needs a father and I know how you feel about marriage but you need a husband. Hear me out—' He put a hand up to stop her as she bristled. 'It can be in name only, or you know we can keep the physical side going since we've both enjoyed it. What I'm saying is, love doesn't have to enter the equation. I don't expect it to. But I have a house you and the baby can live in, I can provide for you, and your reputation remains intact.' He looked so pleased with himself as he shredded her heart into tiny irreparable pieces.

The man she'd apparently never stopped loving, the father of her unborn child, was offering her a marriage of convenience. It somehow seemed worse than the arranged marriages her father had proposed to maintain his social status. Probably because she knew she was in love with Nate and she'd ruined her chances of him ever feeling the same way about her. It was the reason she'd made certain she would leave the country again for London, a place she'd hoped to be able to forget him. Now she would have a permanent reminder.

Nate would always do the right thing, that was who he was, and it was the only reason he *would* want to marry her. She'd wreaked havoc in his life once too often and it wasn't fair to lumber him with a wife and child he'd never wanted. Neither did she want to give up her job to fake a happy marriage, following in her mother's tragic footsteps after all.

In an ideal world her baby would have two doting parents, madly in love with each other, providing the happy, family environment she'd never had. Marrying Nate would simply be perpetuating that myth that money and good name were all that mattered. She would rather raise this baby alone than with a father who was only there out of a sense of duty. The next generation of Dempseys deserved more after the trouble she'd caused to emancipate herself from society rules in the first place.

'It wouldn't work, Nate. We'd only end up making each other miserable. Marriage isn't for us. It's for people who love each other and are willing to give up everything to be together. Forget about me, forget about the baby, and just pretend I never came back. That this never happened.'

The vertigo was back, her head spinning with snapshots of these weeks they'd spent together and memories of her parents' tumultuous relationship. Neither of them should have to compromise who they were simply because they'd made a mistake. In her case, it was falling in love with a man who could never love her back after everything she'd done to him.

'That's impossible.' Nate rested his hand gently on her stomach, staking a claim on the life growing inside her.

She slapped it away. It would be easier for him to walk away now before this was about more than a bunch of cells. 'Not if I'm in a different country. I don't want you in my life, Nate. That wasn't the deal.'

She was shaking with nerves as the lie left her lips, hoping he couldn't see through it, or if he did he'd realise this was her way of letting him off the hook. She wanted Nate in her life more than anything but not through a sense of responsibility. This was her way of trying to protect him, sacrificing her desires again and putting him first before her own needs. No matter how much it hurt.

Violet had taken a sledgehammer to what was left of his heart and pounded it until it was nothing but a big red stain he would never be able to scrub away. He was willing to give himself to her body and soul, something he'd never thought he would do, something he'd never imagined he would *want* to do. Everything he had worked to achieve seemed to have been building up to this moment and asking Violet to share it with him and their baby. Yet, she still didn't want him. The house, the job, the car—none of it was enough to convince her to be with him. None of it seemed to matter without her.

'I know this wasn't what either of us had planned but I'm simply trying to make the best of the situation.' He was doing his damnedest not to get too emotional and make her even more skittish than she was. She didn't respond well to intense personal discussion, as he'd found out to his cost. Her default setting was to run and hide rather than confront the truth; he'd seen it so many times before. She'd disappeared for twelve years after one kiss between them and he knew if she went back this time he'd lose her for ever.

'I just want you to go, Nate.' She sounded tired, resigned to life as a single parent already and he was being forced into the role of absent father. He didn't want to make things even more difficult for Violet than they already were by arguing with her, even though he was dying inside with every push further away. Neither could he, in good conscience, simply walk away after getting her into this condition in the first place.

He wanted to be there as she blossomed during her pregnancy, see their baby on the screen as it happened, not in some grainy printout he'd been sent as an afterthought. That role of a supportive father was important to him. It was something neither of them had really had growing up. Violet's father had been more concerned with his place in society than her feelings and Nate's parents' priority had always been Strachmore.

His childhood hadn't been carefree either, but an endless round of chores and lectures on being respectful. He'd practically had to make himself invisible so as not to offend the Earl. That wasn't conducive to making a child feel wanted or loved. More like an unpaid, unappreciated skivvy. Perhaps if they'd both been accepted for who they were by their own families they wouldn't have the problems they had connecting now.

If Violet didn't want him in her life there wasn't much he could do, but he had to at least try to be a part of their child's. That wasn't going to work long distance and he was willing to make sacrifices to get her to stay if it prevented their baby becoming another statistic of a broken relationship.

'I'll go and I promise not to come back unless you want me to. On the condition you stay at Strachmore until you're due back at work. I want you to be one hundred per cent sure that this is what you want.' His feet were blocks of wood, heavy and clumsy, as he reluctantly made his way to the door. He'd thought knowing she was leaving would be easier than finding out after she'd gone. He was wrong. However, whenever it happened, Violet walking out of his life was always going to be the worst thing that would ever happen to him.

'I am.' She threw one last knife into his back and killed the last dregs of hope stone dead.

CHAPTER NINE

'I'M SURE IT won't be much longer now.' Violet tried to pacify her father, who'd already picked up and set down the one magazine sitting on the waiting-room table. She understood how difficult it was to manage time when dealing with emotional patients, but she also knew how much of a short fuse her father had when he was kept waiting for an appointment. Especially when grief counselling wasn't something he was totally on board with.

He checked the clock again and gave a huff but at least nothing had been thrown in the interim. It was progress but she was still tense sitting here in the hospital with him. Her heart picked up the pace again as the thought of bumping into Nate came to mind. It had been over a week since she'd seen him at the house. He'd kept to his word to stay away as she'd known he would, enabling her to spend her last few days at Strachmore trying to figure out her next move.

'I haven't seen Nathaniel for a while. Did something happen between you two?' Her father picked up on the very subject matter making her unhappy.

Although she was glad he'd chosen conversation over berating the staff to fill the time, every time she thought of telling him about the baby her heart fluttered in her chest and she felt as though she might pass out.

'He's a busy man and we've probably taken up too much of his time at Strachmore.' She had no wish to take up any more of it by making him pay for her mistake. Whether she stayed at home or went back to London, she had to plan the rest of her life without him in it. The thought alone made her light-headed.

'I'm not blind, Violet, nor am I stupid. That boy has been in love with you for years and vice versa, unless I'm very much mistaken. He's hardly been away from Strachmore these past weeks and I doubt that's solely because of me. Now, he's suddenly incommunicado. Something clearly happened between the two of you and, whatever it is, I don't want it to affect your decisions about coming home in the future. I know I drove you away in the past but I really want you to at least visit.'

It was a huge step for him to admit his past behaviour towards her and let her know he wanted her to be part of his life again but, oh, how she wished he were right about Nate's feelings for her. He might have been in love with her when they were kids but time and distance, not to mention her actions, had changed that. She fidgeted with the sleeve of her shirt, knowing she in turn should be honest with him, regardless of how petrified she was at the prospect of having to tell him she was pregnant. He might have mellowed slightly since his heart attack and subsequent procedures but that didn't mean his principles had changed.

The Earl's daughter was pregnant by the son of the housekeeper and it didn't get much more scandalous than that when it came to society gossip. This would be a real test of his priorities but she couldn't put it off much longer. Her condition would soon become apparent if she did come back in the future. It wouldn't be fair on her father to disappear again without telling him why.

She took a deep breath. And another. 'I'm pregnant.'

She braced herself for the backlash—shouting, screaming, crashing furniture—all of his typical reactions to such news would be justified this time. Most of them she'd done herself since sending Nate away.

'And he's not stepping up to his responsibilities?' Only when he'd jumped to the wrong conclusion did his face take on that red hue of impending rage.

'No. It's not that…he even offered to marry me.' She was quick to defend Nate; he'd done everything right. Except love her.

'What's the problem, then?'

'I don't want to get married because it's the right thing to do. I'm sorry, but I'd rather be on my own than in a cold marriage put on for appearances' sake.' Her reasons for turning Nate down might seem a tad insensitive in light of the present situation but it was the truth. Perhaps if there'd been a bit more of that between her parents, or between her and Nate, things could've turned out much differently. If she'd been honest with him about the strength of her feelings for him in the first place they might've actually stood a chance together.

Her father's frown turned into a half-smile. 'Marriage always was your sticking point. That doesn't mean you can't still be together. Times have changed, so you keep telling me.'

She was surprised he'd paid any heed to her word against that of his ingrained sense of tradition. An illegitimate child would have devastated him not so long ago but he was clearly working hard on keeping their relationship alive.

'I can't be with someone who doesn't love me. It wouldn't be fair on me, or the baby.' She rubbed her hand over her still flat-belly, wishing only happiness for the life growing inside her.

'I don't believe that for one minute. Only a man in love would put up with your irritable father and do everything he has to secure Strachmore's future. I think it's *you* who doesn't want to commit.'

'Well, he's never said it,' she huffed, upset at the accusation she was the one at fault here. As far as she was concerned she'd done everything right to ensure Nate had been treated fairly. Not many women would've given him the green light to walk away. Especially when they were head over heels about him and carrying his child.

'Have *you*? You know, if I could change things I'd make sure your mother and I had really talked about how we felt. I'd make damn sure I listened. Don't throw something special away because you're scared to face the truth. You'll spend the rest of your life regretting it.' His teary blue eyes were a reflection of her own but she feared they'd both left it too late. She'd pushed Nate away, said some horrible things to ensure he'd stay out of her life. Unfortunately, given his silence since, she seemed to have succeeded in her quest.

'You're not mad at me? About the baby?' She was going to need at least one person to be there holding her hand when this bundle of trouble arrived and turned everything upside down. If she had her father's support it would ease some of her stress and help her enjoy this pregnancy more. So far it had been all tension and sickness and she was still waiting for the so-called blossoming to start.

He sighed.

'It's not what I wanted for you but it's not the end of the world. I just want you to be happy.' He reached over and gave her hand a squeeze, the only loving gesture she could ever remember getting from him. She cursed her hormones as the tears tipped over the edge of her lashes. She wasn't sure she'd ever be truly happy again.

'Lord Dempsey?' The receptionist called him for his appointment, drawing them both out of their heart-to-heart and on their feet.

'Whoa.' Violet had to sit down again as all the blood in her body seemed to rush to her head at once.

The receptionist rushed over to check on her. 'Are you all right?'

'She's pregnant,' her father answered for her, rubbing her back, already playing the role of protective grandfather.

'Just a little dizzy. My heart's racing a little but that's been happening a lot recently.' She didn't want to make a fuss and somehow have Nate get wind of it, but she was a bit breathless and seriously feeling as if she was about to faint.

'At least you're in the right place. I'll put in a call and get them to check you out in A and E.'

Violet could only nod as she struggled to stay conscious.

It wasn't long before she found herself stretched out on a bed with electrodes stuck all over her body, hooked up to an ECG machine. They'd gone over her medical history, and taken blood samples. She didn't know what they were expecting to find but the longer she lay here worrying what was happening, the faster her heart rate seemed to get. It was beating so hard she could easily have just finished running a marathon rather than simply have had an intense conversation with her father. She rested her hands on her invisible bump. It was still early days into her pregnancy and she was trying not to freak out about the fact she was already in hospital.

The doctor studied the printout of her test with a frown, which wasn't helping her relax at all. 'Your heart rate is higher than we would like. At the minute it's beating so fast the heart muscle can't relax between contractions and the lack of oxygen is what's causing the dizzy spells.'

'Will it harm the baby?' That was all that mattered right now. She mightn't have planned on this baby but neither did she want anything to happen to it. It was all she had left of Nate now.

He shook his head. 'There's nothing to worry about. We do want to send you to CCU, though, so they can keep a close eye on you during treatment.'

If she didn't laugh at the irony she'd cry. It was the one department in the building she was virtually guaranteed to see the man she'd been trying to avoid. There was no way her baby daddy was going to remain a silent partner once she and junior rocked up on his turf. He was going to have plenty to say about looking after herself and his child. Fate was going to make sure they had one last showdown before she left for London this time.

London. It had been her salvation, her road to independence, but now going back to her empty apartment felt like a punishment for her mistake. She had family here, and friends. And Nate. All she had in London was her job. She'd been so busy building walls to protect her heart she'd isolated herself emotionally and physically from anyone who'd tried to get close. It wasn't the ideal set-up for a woman raising a child on her own. What if there were any more complications during the pregnancy? She had no one to lean on there because that was the way she'd wanted it. Impending motherhood had since changed her views on complete independence.

These past weeks had reminded her how good it felt to have companionship, to be loved, to be *in* love. Even having her father waiting patiently outside for news she and the baby were safe was a turning point in their relationship, an insight into the family life she could have had here. Returning to a one-bedroom flat, pregnant and broken-hearted, wasn't something she was looking forward to. She was going to miss Strachmore and everyone associated with it.

Nate was on his way to do the rounds on the coronary care unit, having just finished fitting a pacemaker for one of his patients. It was best to keep busy to stop him from running up to Strachmore to see if Violet was still there. He'd given her his word he wouldn't go near her to give her space to think, but the distinct lack of communication indicated his plan to get her to stick around had backfired. As she'd told him in no uncertain terms, she didn't want, or need, him in her life. He didn't even know if she was still in the country.

This time he wasn't simply going to accept her decision. He would follow her to London if it meant he could at least see their child grow and flourish. Without Violet and the baby here he wasn't sure what was keeping him here anyway. The house he'd been so proud of owning now seemed too big for a single man, too empty. The rooms should be full of toys and plans for the future, not a reminder of everything he'd lost. He didn't know how he was ever going to get over her this time, knowing what they could have...*should* have had together. Too bad his peasant status had let him down again. It was a stigma he would never be able to overcome to become worthy of the Earl's daughter. Or perhaps he'd simply have to face the fact that she'd never loved him anyway and he'd been the one using his upbringing as an excuse. Either way she didn't want him, and he was lost without her.

If only it were as easy to fix his broken heart as those of his patients. He'd gladly volunteer as a guinea pig for any new research looking into replacing emotionally battered hearts if it meant an end to this misery. He hadn't even been able to share the pain of losing the woman he loved and his baby when no one had known they'd existed, including his family. This was only supposed to have been a meaningless fling; there'd been no reason to broadcast the fact they were together. He'd had no way of knowing this would change him for ever. Somehow he was going to have to break the news to his parents they were soon to become grandparents and they might never see their first, and possibly only, grandchild.

Thoughts of Violet and the baby had tormented him for days; he'd been wondering if some day another man would take over *his* role as husband and father.

He knew without doubt he could never replace what he'd lost, but that didn't mean Violet wouldn't love someone else, someone acceptable. If she didn't relent about seeing him again to at least discuss future arrangements, he might have to move away too. He didn't think he could face Strachmore again or hearing any stories coming out of it. He'd been here before, knew the pain he'd go through to come out the other side and the only thing to get him through was hard work.

In fact he was obsessing over his personal life so much it was encroaching on his professional one. He would've sworn he'd seen the Earl walk past when the CCU doors had flashed open at the end of the corridor. Impossible. He would've known if his patient had been readmitted. Still, it would put his mind at rest to check with the senior nurse in charge.

'Has Samuel Dempsey been admitted again, by any chance?'

'No, but he's here with his daughter. She came in yesterday.'

'What? Why didn't anyone tell me?' In the fearful haze clouding his brain he'd forgotten this had been a secret affair. His colleagues had no idea this woman in jeopardy was everything to him.

The nurse frowned. 'She said she didn't want us to contact anyone. We've put her in Room One—'

Nate didn't wait to hear any more. He was already haring off to find Violet, regardless of whether she wanted to see him or not. People weren't admitted to CCU on a whim, especially pregnant women. If Violet, or the baby, were in danger he was going to be there for them regardless of her objections.

He burst into the side room and, while he was glad

to see her again, the sight of her lying in the hospital bed, small and pale, was almost his undoing. The heart monitors that were part of his everyday job now took on a sinister new meaning as they charted her progress.

'Nate!'

Perhaps he should have given her some warning before crashing in here as he watched her heart rate spike on the screen. He reached for her charts to find out exactly what was going on. 'Are you and the baby okay?'

'We're fine. I didn't sleep very well last night so they moved me in here for a little more peace and quiet.' Despite the circumstances and how they'd left things the last time they'd seen each other, she actually looked pleased to see him.

'Why didn't you phone me?' He directed his question at her father, sitting by the bedside, not a figment of his imagination at all. It was more of an accusation that he'd been purposely kept out of the loop. Probably by the man who'd made it his life's work to interfere in hers. So much for the new leaf they'd supposed he'd turned over.

'I told him not to. I've caused you enough grief over the years. It's not fair to keep involving you in my problems.' Violet's admission saved him from beginning a new battle with her father even though it was completely without foundation. He'd never backed away when she'd needed him.

'Why not? This is my baby too. I *want* to be involved.' A second too late he realised he'd blown the big secret. She might not have wanted her father to know her predicament before she'd gone back to London and now Nate would have his reaction on his conscience too.

'As I told her you should be. Now, I think it's about time you two had a serious talk about your future, about this baby.' The Earl's lack of punch-throwing and willingness to walk out of the room, leaving him alone with his daughter, led Nate to believe Violet had already broken the news of the addition to the family.

'You told him?'

'I didn't think I'd be able to hide it much longer. He took it better than I could ever have dreamed of.'

'Clearly. I'm still standing.' It would've been a different story twelve years ago, pre medical school, if he'd knocked up the Earl's daughter. The long road to cardiology had been worth it to be accepted on some level, if not as part of the family.

'Actually, he didn't seem that surprised. I guess we weren't as discreet as we thought we'd been.' That twinkle in her eye took Nate back to a time and a place he was already having trouble letting go of.

'Okay. Let's see what we have here.' He resisted running over and kissing her when he knew for sure she wasn't in immediate danger. It might be pushing his luck too far.

SVT, supraventricular tachycardia, was something he'd had plenty of experience with in his patients, including pregnant women. The complications that could arise were often due to the presence of heart disease, a cause for concern given her father's recent history. Thankfully her ultrasounds and ECGs had ruled this out. She had, however, been admitted with a very high tachycardia rate, reaching between one hundred and eighty and two hundred and forty beats per minute.

'I'm fine, honestly.' Violet tried to convince him

there was no need for him to worry, or be here, but he could see her arrhythmia had not yet abated.

'We still need to get that heart rate stable again before you leave.' There was no way she was going home until he knew all was well. A beta blocker had already been administered to no avail. There was always a small chance the administered drugs could cross the placental barrier so it wasn't something he wanted for her long term when there were no obvious benefits in her case. The alternative wasn't something he relished for the mother of his unborn child either.

'They said they might have to take me to Theatre?' There was a slight tremor in her voice belying her nerves even though she was insisting on her indestructability.

Since she hadn't bawled at him to get out of the room he dared to get closer to the bedside. 'If your heart rate doesn't regulate they are planning electrical cardioversion. Essentially this will be delivering a mild electric shock to jolt the heart back into a normal rhythm.'

'The same thing you did to Dad?'

'Something similar. Except without the drama. And you're a much prettier patient.' He couldn't stop himself from reaching out and stroking her hair back from her forehead. This could be the last time he'd see her if she chose life in London alone over one with him. The last chance he had to tell her how he really felt in the hope it could somehow make a difference.

She closed her eyes. 'Nate—'

'You scared me, you know. When they told me you were here I nearly flipped my lid. I know you don't want to hear it but I want to marry you. I want to raise our baby together. I don't want to find out what's happening to you via a third party.' There were eight months left of this pregnancy, never mind the next eighteen years of their baby's life.

'I appreciate the sentiment but a marriage of convenience isn't what I want. It never has been. Forcing you to marry someone you don't love makes me no better than my father when he was trying to pair me off for the greater good. I don't expect you to make compromises in your life to suit me, nor am I willing to do that for anyone. I saw what that did to my mother.'

'I'm not asking you to make compromises. I'm simply asking you to be with me. And what's this nonsense about not loving you? I've loved you since our private prom night in the boathouse and I doubt I'll ever stop loving you. You're the one who keeps running out on me.' He wasn't about to take responsibility for her fleeing the country again when he was the one trying to get her to stay. If she was insisting on leaving because the thought of being with him was so abhorrent, he wanted to hear her say it. It was the only way he was ever going to be able to accept it.

'But…but…you made it sound as though you felt an obligation to marry me. You never mentioned the L word.' Violet held her breath, the impact of what he was saying too great to comprehend in her current state. He was basically killing her argument for getting on a plane back to London stone dead.

'The last time I did that you disappeared for over a decade. I was trying to prevent another vanishing-woman act. Listen, I know I didn't measure up then and no amount of certificates will make me a qualified member of the aristocracy, but I will look after you and our child. I don't want you to change. I'm not asking anything from you except to give us a chance.'

She thought her heart was going to burst through her chest, it felt so full. Nate loved her; even after everything, he loved her.

'I was scared, that's why I left the first time, why I was leaving now. I thought it was best for you. I watched my parents' love turn to hate with the pressures of society. I didn't want that for you, or us. The strength of my feelings for you was never in question but I didn't want it to be at the cost of anyone's freedom. You didn't sign up for a baby, or a grumpy Earl, or a run-down country estate.' It said a lot that he was still here now she'd reminded him of all the baggage she was lugging with her.

Nate sat on the edge of the bed and took her hand in his. 'I love you. Everything else we can deal with.'

She didn't think she'd ever get tired of hearing him say those words. 'You mean it?'

'I mean every word. I want to marry you because I love you. A baby is just the icing on the cake. I'll move to London with you, leave my job and be a stay-at-home dad, whatever it takes for us to be together because that's what I want more than anything else in the world.' He leaned over and placed a gentle kiss on her lips.

As soon as he touched her the tension left her body, a sense of peace finally descending and releasing her from the burdens of the past. This was everything she'd been waiting for.

After a long, satisfying smooch, Nate got up from the bed. 'I don't believe it.'

'What?'

He was staring at the heart monitor and she automatically feared the worst. No matter who tried to reassure her, having electrodes stuck to her body to conduct electricity to her organs wasn't how a first-time mum wanted to begin her pregnancy. She'd take morning sickness or a craving for pickles over that scenario any day.

'Your heart rate is stabilising on its own.'

Violet followed his gaze. Sure enough the figures were dropping, evening out to where they were supposed to be. Finding Nate *actually* wanted to marry her had been enough to shock her heart into working properly again. Although, she might have to insist he keep his distance for a while longer. If he kept kissing her and things got steamy there was every chance he'd send her pulse sky-high again.

'In that case I guess we can start making plans for the future. We've got a baby to think about.'

She didn't want to spend any more time looking back. Not when she had so much to look forward to. Her life was going to change for ever, probably bring more challenges along the way, but with Nate at her side she knew she could face them head-on.

After all, one kiss from him had been enough to heal her heart.

EPILOGUE

VIOLET WATCHED FROM her bedroom window as the wedding guests filed around the side of the house to the Victorian conservatory. This was it, the day she'd fought against for most of her life in the very place she'd run from as a teenager and she couldn't have been happier. In less than an hour's time she'd be marrying Nate.

With Strachmore now fully licensed to hold weddings, it seemed fitting that theirs would be the first. They'd agreed upon a small affair with only close family and friends in attendance, simple and discreet with none of the palaver she'd always associated with society weddings. Today was about celebrating their love and nothing else. Everything was perfect.

She stroked her small baby bump concealed under her white lace bridal gown. It wouldn't be long before the three of them would become a family. The past four months had been a whirlwind of activity. After a great deal of thought she'd decided she wanted to move back to Northern Ireland, with both families nearby when the baby arrived. Nate had gone with her back to London to help her pack her things for moving in with him while she worked out her notice. With all of their pre-planning she hoped the rest of her pregnancy was going to be more relaxing.

Once the baby was born she would go back to work at a local level and share the childminding with Nate and the excited grandparents anxiously awaiting the new arrival. Everything was slotting into place. She just wished she had her mother here to share it.

A knock on the door interrupted her maudlin thoughts before they could fully develop and taint the happiest day of her life.

'I just wanted to see how my beautiful bride was holding up.' Nate, devastatingly handsome in his wedding tuxedo, stepped into the room and immediately lifted her spirits again. She couldn't help but wonder if he wore one of those mood rings she'd had as a kid, which had some way of telling him when she needed him most.

'I'm fine, but isn't it bad luck for us to see each other before the wedding?' She really didn't want to tempt fate when it had taken so long for them to reach this point.

'I thought we'd broken free of tradition and superstition by now? These days we make our own luck.' He crossed the room in three strides to reach her and slip his hands around her waist. It was all she needed to feel complete again.

'You're right. I'm sure there's a million women out there who'd want to swap places with me at this moment.' She was the luckiest woman alive to be marrying this man today and she wasn't going to let any imagined curses get in the way of that a second time.

'Have I told you how stunning you are yet? I have to keep pinching myself as a reminder that this is actually happening.' He deflected her comment with one of his own, standing back to admire her vintage-style dress.

'This is *actually* happening. We're minutes away from taking our vows in front of all those people out there.' The nerves started to creep back in at the thought of leaving this lovely cosy cocoon with Nate and proclaiming their love in public.

'Well, we've got a little while yet…' He had that twinkle in his eye that said *NT* wanted to make his mark one last time as a single man.

'Do you know how long it took for me to squeeze into this dress? There's no way I'm taking it off again.' The knowledge he still found her irresistible despite her changing body was enough to send shivers of need skating across her skin and make her want to fast-forward to their wedding night.

'Who said anything about getting you naked? Honestly, the way your hormones are raging I'm wondering if I'm going to make it back from the honeymoon alive.' His fake outrage widened Violet's smile even further. She couldn't promise him that when they were going to spend the next two weeks alone on a tropical island. They were still making up for lost time.

'So if you're not going to seduce me, what are you doing in my bedroom, Mr Taylor?'

'I have a present for you, soon-to-be Mrs Taylor.' Nate reached into his pocket and pulled out a small velvet jewellery box. He opened it to reveal a delicate silver necklace.

'It's beautiful.' Violet fingered the tiny diamond-encrusted entwined seahorses dangling from the end of the chain he was now fastening around her neck.

She'd taken off her bracelet today and had felt naked without it, as if a piece of her were missing.

'I'm afraid I couldn't get your mother's necklace back for you, but I thought you could do with an upgrade from my last gift of jewellery.'

'Thank you.' She knew this was his way of marking the start of their new life together and fading out the past.

'I thought we could have our first dance here too. Without anyone else.' He placed her hands around his neck and took her in his arms. She closed her eyes and relaxed into his embrace, remembering their faux prom where they'd danced in secret and fallen in love for the first time. Nate was all she'd ever needed.

As they held each other tight, their bodies swaying together with nothing but the beat of their hearts keeping time, Violet knew there was nowhere else she'd rather be. She'd finally come home.

* * * * *

*If you enjoyed this story, check out
these other great reads from Karin Baine*

*A KISS TO CHANGE HER LIFE
FRENCH FLING TO FOREVER*

Available now!

MILLS & BOON®

MEDICAL ROMANCE™

THE ULTIMATE IN ROMANTIC MEDICAL DRAMA

Lynne Graham has sold 35 million books!

To settle a debt, she'll have to become his mistress…

Nikolai Drakos is determined to have his revenge against the man who destroyed his sister. So stealing his enemy's intended fiancé seems like the perfect solution! Until Nikolai discovers that woman is Ella Davies…

Read on for a tantalising excerpt from Lynne Graham's 100th book,

BOUGHT FOR THE GREEK'S REVENGE

'Mistress,' Nikolai slotted in cool as ice.

Shock had welded Ella's tongue to the roof of her mouth because he was sexually propositioning her and nothing could have prepared her for that. She wasn't drop-dead gorgeous… *he* was! Male heads didn't swivel when Ella walked down the street because she had neither the length of leg nor the curves usually deemed necessary to attract such attention. Why on earth could he be making *her* such an offer?

'But we don't even know each other,' she framed dazedly. 'You're a stranger…'

'If you live with me I won't be a stranger for long,' Nikolai pointed out with monumental calm. And the very sound of that inhuman calm and cool forced her to flip round and settle distraught eyes on his lean darkly handsome face.

'You can't be serious about this!'

'I assure you that I am deadly serious. Move in and I'll forget your family's debts.'

'But it's a *crazy* idea!' she gasped.

'It's not crazy to me,' Nikolai asserted. 'When I want anything, I go after it hard and fast.'

Her lashes dipped. Did he want her like that? Enough to track her down, buy up her father's debts, and try and buy rights to her and her body along with those debts? The very idea of that made her dizzy and plunged her brain into even greater turmoil. 'It's immoral… it's blackmail.'

'It's definitely *not* blackmail. I'm giving you the benefit of a choice you didn't have before I came through that door,' Nikolai Drakos fielded with a glittering cool. 'That choice is yours to make.'

'Like hell it is!' Ella fired back. 'It's a complete cheat of a supposed offer!'

Nikolai sent her a gleaming sideways glance. 'No the real cheat was you kissing me the way you did last year and then saying no and acting as if I had grossly insulted you,' he murmured with lethal quietness.

'You *did* insult me!' Ella flung back, her cheeks hot as fire while she wondered if her refusal that night had started off his whole chain reaction. What else could possibly be driving him?

Nikolai straightened lazily as he opened the door. 'If you take offence that easily, maybe it's just as well that the answer is no.'

MILLS & BOON®

Mills & Boon have been at the heart of romance since 1908… and while the fashions may have changed, one thing remains the same: from pulse-pounding passion to the gentlest caress, we're always known how to bring romance alive.

Now, we're delighted to present you with these irresistible illustrations, inspired by the vintage glamour of our covers. So indulge your wildest dreams and unleash your imagination as we present the most iconic Mills & Boon moments of the last century.

Visit **www.millsandboon.co.uk/ArtofRomance** to order yours!